2003 Happy
Now you
aspect of "Country music.
Love, Carolyn

Redneck Liberation

Country Music as Theology

*Jim,
Thanks for all you do and all you mean to our church!*

Dick Gillig

Redneck Liberation

Country Music as Theology

David Fillingim

Mercer University Press
Macon, Georgia

ISBN   0-86554-841-2 (hardback)
       0-86554-896-X (paperback)
MUP/   H634
       P263

© 2003 Mercer University Press
6316 Peake Road
Macon, Georgia 31210-3960
All rights reserved

First Edition.

∞The paper used in this publication meets the minimum requirements of American National Standard for Information Sciences—Permanence of Paper for Printed Library Materials, ANSI Z39.48-1992.

Library of Congress Cataloging-in-Publication Data

Fillingim, David, 1960-
Redneck liberation : country music as theology / David Fillingim.--
1st ed.
    p. cm.
Includes bibliographical references and index.
ISBN 0-86554-841-2 (alk. paper)—ISBN 0-86554-896-X (pbk. : alk. paper)
1. Country music—Religious aspects. I. Title.
ML3524.F55 2003
781.642--dc21
                                                        2003012059

Contents

Introduction:
    Honky-Tonkology:
    Taking Country Music Seriously   1

1. The Gospel Songs and the Cheatin' Songs:
    Suffering and the Failure of Redneck Theology   23

2. The Gospel According to Hank:
    Country Music's Hillbilly Humanist Moral Core   43

3. The Apocalypse According to Garth:
    Riding toward the Postmodern Roundup   69

4. Stand by Your Man and Your Daughters Shall Prophesy:
    The Emergence of Honky-Tonk Feminism   101

Epilogue:
    All I Really Need to Know I Learned from
    Country Music   141

Bibliography   157

Index   163

To Malinda, Hope, and Hannah

Acknowledgments

This book has been a long time in the making. I began researching and writing about country music as theology in the Fall of 1994. So many people have encouraged and influenced me during the writing of this book that I couldn't possibly name them all. So I apologize at the outset to those I leave out.

Some of the material in this book appeared in different form in two articles in the journal Studies in Popular Culture, published by the Popular Culture Association in the South/American Culture Association in the South (PCAS/ACAS). I'd like to thank the editors of that journal-first Dennis Hall and then Michael and Sara Dunne-for their enthusiasm and encouragement. PCAS/ACAS has been a fun and fruitful forum in which to develop my thinking on the topic over the years.

I'd also like to thank B. W. Aston, editor of the West Texas Historical Association Year Book, and the good folks at Sojourners magazine for publishing earlier versions of some of the ideas contained herein.

On separate occasions, Ronnie Pugh and Elak Horvath at the Country Music Foundation assisted with discographic and bibliographic details.

Marc Jolley of Mercer University Press has been an enthusiastic and patient supporter of this project.

And I'd like especially to thank my wife, Malinda, and my daughters, Hope and Hannah, for sometimes sharing and sometimes tolerating my love of country music, and to apologize to them for those times when I've caused our lives together to resemble a country song a little too closely.

Introduction

Honky-Tonkology: Taking Country Music Seriously

> It is a source of deep historical confusion to identify the history of Christian morality with the record of the thoughts of academic moralists.... The relation between the academic articulation and the real life of the community is more like that of the froth to the beer.[1]
>
> —John Howard Yoder

> You got to have smelt a lot of mule manure before you can sing like a hillbilly....What he is singing is the hopes and prayers and dreams of what some call the common people.[2]
>
> —Hank Williams

---

[1] John Howard Yoder, *When War Is Unjust: Being Honest in Just War Thinking* (Minneapolis: Augsburg Publishing House, 1984) 73.

[2] Quoted in Curtis Ellison, *Country Music Culture: From Hard Times to Heaven* (Jackson: University Press of Mississippi, 1995) 107.

In country music, things aren't always exactly what they seem. "Hillbilly" singers dress like cowboys, even if they've never actually been within spitting distance of the open range. Country music personalities claim in all seriousness to be preserving the music's pure, simple, down-home roots through elaborate stage and video productions in the context of a multi-billion dollar industry utilizing state of the art technologies in recording, producing, and merchandizing their products. Imagine sitting on the porch of Grandma's log cabin wired to the web for Reba's live on-line chat and music video broadcast. Images surrounding country music are sometimes incongruous, sometimes downright misleading.

And so it is with country music scholarship. Take, for example, the title of this introduction. My use of the term "honky-tonk" is somewhat misleading, since honky-tonk is a subgenre of country music to which I have not narrowly confined my focus either here or in the rest of the book. But I am not the first academic interpreter of country music to employ inaccurate or misleading terms for the sake of good-sounding titles. A burgeoning academic literature in popular culture studies includes a number of recent books on country music. Historians, sociologists, and literary critics have weighed in with their interpretations of what is often considered the most loathsome of musical styles. So why am I putting in my two cents worth? And what do I mean by suggesting, in the title of this book, that country music is somehow "theology"?

Theomusicology: Popular Music as Theology

John Michael Spencer argues that all popular music is theological and has coined the term theomusicology to denote his approach to interpreting musical traditions. Popular music is theological, Spencer says, because religion is "all-pervasive in culture." People are "inescapably" and naturally religious; we naturally ask and reflect on ultimate questions. Popular music reveals how people "ponder myriad vital questions that arise out of our sense of finiteness." In sacred or church music, "provisional answers to the vital questions are already narrowly predetermined" by doctrinal and ecclesial necessity. Therefore, popular music provides a truer window into the human soul and reveals "a more honest religious discourse." Popular music reflects the religious imagination unfettered by the chains of doctrinal propriety.[3]

Spencer, whose research focuses on the blues and other African-American musical traditions, provides further theoretical grounds for elaborating Curtis Ellison's recognition that country music is inherently theological. According to Ellison, romantic love and gospel salvation function in country music as parallel paths "from hard times to heaven."[4] In fact, these sacred and secular paths are not parallel, but overlapping. Songs like Ricochet's "Her Daddy's Money" and Sammy Kershaw's "Vidalia" signify the connection between romance and salvation by making church

---

[3] John Michael Spencer, "Overview of American Popular Music in a Theological Perspective," *Black Sacred Music* 8/1 (Spring 1994): 205–206, 216.

[4] Curtis Ellison, *Country Music Culture: From Hard Times to Heaven* (Jackson: University Press of Mississippi, 1995).

the location of the romantic encounter, while Rick Trevino takes advantage of dual meanings of the word "save," praying that his own romantic desire might supercede the desired woman's religious experience in "Save This One for Me."

In many country songs, the spiritual serves as a metaphor for the sexual, and vice versa. The Kendalls sing "Heaven's Just a Sin Away." T. G. Sheppard recounts how his illicit lover whispers the same invitation that the preacher shouted from the creek bank: "Do You Want to Go to Heaven?" Mel McDaniel adopts a gospel pose, exhorting his congregation to "Testify" about a backseat rendezvous. Daryle Singletary praises an "Amen Kind of Love," while Randy Travis promises a love that will last "Forever and Ever, Amen." Alan Jackson notes the saving power and ultimate significance of romantic love: his mate is the only thing standing "Between the Devil and Me." In "Water into Wine," Patty Loveless alludes to Jesus' first miracle to note the scope of the impact of the romance she has found.

But the ultimate power of romantic love cuts both ways. Hank Williams, George Jones, and others have built their repertoires around the devastation caused by love gone wrong, lending credence to country music's reputation as misery set to music. Bluegrass great Del McCoury captures the link between lost love and lost religion in "Backslidin' Blues": "I've quit goin' to church, and gone back to sinnin'/ Since you put me out with the trash." In country music as in the blues, romantic love serves as a crucible in which one can encounter the ultimate and either be transformed or destroyed.

Anthony Pinn steps beyond Spencer's theomusicological interpretive approach and argues for a "nitty-gritty hermeneutics" that looks honestly and unabashedly at the ways blues, rap, and other musical forms express and respond to the raw experience of suffering and evil. Pinn faults theistic interpretations like Spencer's and Cone's as tautological: they find that the blues are theological precisely because they presume the existence of God as ultimate concern. An honest, nitty-gritty hermeneutic reveals, Pinn argues, that the blues deny God's existence and promote a version of humanism—the ontological and moral ultimacy of the human. Humans, not God, are seen as responsible for evil and for resisting evil. In other words, the blues are not theology but anti-theology.[5]

While I will suggest that country music at times embodies a rejection of specific theological categories emphasized in white gospel music, to argue that country music is atheistic would be impossible. As expressed on a popular bumper sticker, a curious amalgam of "God, guns, and guts" is endemic to country music's cultural context. The songs one hears on country radio are sprinkled with references to God and to Christian tradition as pervasive as flakes of pepper in a bowl of grits. If Pinn is correct that the blues are atheistic, then how can country music in any meaningful way be seen as the "white man's blues"? I would suggest that a broader, more fluid understanding of what constitutes "theology" is called for when interpreting popular culture texts as theological discourse.

In analyzing country music as theology, I do not intend to claim that country music constructs a Christian theology. In fact, my way of viewing country music as theology does not necessarily even imply theistic belief. In other words, I

---

[5] Anthony Pinn, *Why Lord? Suffering and Evil in Black Theology* (New York: Continuum, 1995) 113–22.

reject the dichotomies sometimes used to define the term "theology"—such as theology vs. religion or theism vs. humanism. In describing country music as theology, I mean simply that country music embodies certain basic beliefs about reality or, to borrow Tillich's often-used phrase, about matters of ultimate concern. A text counts as theological discourse to the extent that it interprets raw experience by (de)constructing systems of order and meaning or to the extent that it relates mundane experience to the perception of ultimate significance or ultimate power. Thus, even if the blues are atheistic, they are still theological because they make statements about matters of ultimate concern. Country music, though usually theistic, is analagous to the blues because both deconstruct narrowly Christian structures of meaning and assert other experiences as ultimate.

In his book *What's the Difference? A Comparison of the Faiths Men Live By*, Louis Cassels writes that one's religion is "the set of assumptions—conscious or unconscious—on which you base your day-to-day decisions and actions."[6] In a religion so broadly defined, theology would be the effort to articulate those assumptions. Country music articulates assumptions that shape the worldview of the group that Hank Williams calls, in the quote at the head of this chapter, "the common people." In other words, country music is the theological self-expression of the hillbilly or redneck.

---

[6] Louis Cassels, *What's the Difference? A Comparison of the Faiths Men Live By* (New York: Doubleday & Company, 1965), reprinted at www.religion-online.org.

The Redneck as a Member of a Marginalized Community

So, who are the "rednecks" (or, to be politically correct, "Agro-Americans")? Comedian Jeff Foxworthy has become wealthy telling, writing, and singing redneck jokes. Because Foxworthy speaks with a pronounced Southern accent, listeners are to recognize that his jokes are not offensive to rural Southerners. But I have serious problems with Foxworthy's jokes. In a series of three published collections of Foxworthy's "You might be a redneck if..." one-liners,[7] we learn that rednecks live in rural areas, have voracious sexual appetites (including desires for incest and bestiality), are uneducated and downright stupid, demonstrate little impulse control, are lazy and shiftless, love their hunting dogs more than their families, are violent and prone to criminal behavior, are alcoholics, own numerous inoperable motor vehicles, and have dangerously poor hygiene. Redneck women are portrayed as disgustingly macho and particularly libidinous. Furthermore, Foxworthy describes "redneck" as "a state of mind," implying that everyone has a bit of redneck inside. In short, Foxworthy's promotion of negative stereotypes, despite his Southern accent, does not contribute to cultural understanding.

Baptist writer, preacher, and native redneck Will D. Campbell provides a better starting point for elaborating redneck identity. Campbell uses the word redneck to refer to

---

[7] Jeff Foxworthy, *You Might Be A Redneck If...*(Atlanta: Longstreet Press, 1989), *Red Ain't Dead: 150 More Ways to Tell If You're a Redneck* (Atlanta: Longstreet Press, 1991), *Check Your Neck: More of You Might Be A Redneck If...* (Atlanta: Longstreet Press, 1992).

"the underprivileged white of mill town and rural South." Rednecks constitute "a less obvious minority" in the American South. The sharecropper system, through which the rednecks eked out a bare existence from the soil, was "a more sneaky kind of slavery, so the redneck never had to acknowledge it."[8] In other words, the redneck has been oppressed without ever realizing it. The interests of the white Southern oligarchy, historically the oppressors of both poor white and poor black, obviously lay in keeping the fear and anger of the two groups of poor Southerners directed at one another rather than at the ruling elite.[9] Throughout the nineteenth century, the life of the poor white rural Southerner was a transient, migratory, and contingent one. Rednecks moved often, seeking a place where they could farm with some measure of success and security. The best lands were consumed by large-scale planters in the plantation economy, so small farmers were forced into ever more remote locations, leaving them in a marginal position socially and economically.[10]

Rednecks have never really moved from this marginal position, geographically or culturally. Stereotyped as ignorant, vilified as racist, and assumed to be privileged simply because they are white, rednecks constantly have been at the margins of Southern society and have often been made scapegoats for the region's perceived shortcomings. Popular derision directed at rednecks transcends limits governing "proper" discourse

---

[8] Will Campbell, "The World of the Redneck," *Katallagate: Journal of the Committee of Southern Churchmen* 5 (Spring): 35–37.

[9] Ibid.; see also Martin Luther King, Jr., *Why We Can't Wait* (New York: Harper & Row, 1963) 36.

[10] Dickson D. Bruce, *And They All Sang Hallelujah: Plain-Folk Camp-Meeting Religion, 1800–1845* (Knoxville: University of Tennessee Press, 1977) 13–24.

when talking about other cultural groups. As "Kentuckian-American," Wendell Berry points out that even among the advocates of political correctness or multiculturalism, negative stereotypes of rural and working-class whites remain fashionable.[11] The rise of an industrial economy made migrants of the rednecks again, as they moved North to urban areas in search of work. The geographic displacement of the redneck community continued by means of the urbanization of the South and the dispersion of rednecks and their culture through military tours of duty. This geographic expansion is perhaps the key factor in the early commercial development of country music. Campbell's "mill town and rural" redneck community had evolved into a redneck diaspora. When folks moved in search of a more bearable life, they carried their musical tastes with them.

So What is Country Music?

Country music was born in 1927 in Bristol, Tennessee. Victor Records sent talent scout and recording engineer Ralph Peer on a tour of the South to seek out new talent. Peer was looking for traditional musicians who could imitate the success of "Old Familiar Tunes" recorded by Fiddlin' John Carson and Vernon Dalhart. The Bristol sessions proved to be the most productive on Peer's itinerary. Jimmie Rodgers, a previously unknown singer then living in Asheville, North Carolina, was one of the acts who showed up in Peer's temporary recording studio. The Carter Family, from nearby

---

[11] Wendell Berry, *Sex, Economy, Freedom & Community* (New York: Pantheon, 1992) xv.

Maces Springs, Virginia, was another. The Carters and Jimmie Rodgers were commercial country music's first star acts. They rose to stardom during the period in which urban migration and military service were spreading "hillbilly" tastes and hillbilly music throughout the country and around the world.

Of course, country music wasn't really "born" at one particular place or time, but the Bristol sessions do represent a crucial moment for the commercial emergence of country music. Country music's roots are heterogeneous—including influences from traditional Appalachian folk ballads, popular parlor songs, the blues, sacred music traditions, minstrelsy, vaudeville, and other sources. Nineteenth-century Southern rural folk music—country music's immediate precursor—is a hybrid that cannot be traced to any pure Celtic or Appalachian tradition or clearly separated from a number of other musical traditions.[12]

Jimmie Rodgers is often regarded as the father of country music. Rodgers grew up in Meridian, Mississippi, an important urban center and railroad junction. He joined a traveling medicine show at age fourteen and had been a vaudeville singer before being "discovered" by Peer in Bristol. As a "hillbilly" singer, Rodgers had precursors. Through the 1920s, operatically trained crooner Vernon Dalhart vied with millhand "Fiddlin' John Carson for the rank of king of the "Old Familiar" tunes, as record companies discovered the commercial appeal of Southern rural music. But it was Rodgers's unique singing style known as the "blue

---

[12] See Bill Malone, *Singing Cowboys and Musical Mountaineers: Southern Culture and the Roots of Country Music* (Athens: University of Georgia Press, 1993).

yodel"—a blend of African-American blues and hillbilly anguish—that would become an object of imitation for succeeding generations of country artists. Among Rodgers's early imitators were Roy Acuff, who would become the first big "star" of the Grand Ole Opry; Gene Autry, who would be the first of the singing cowboy stars; and Hank Williams. Curtis Ellison sees in Rodgers's career the origin of the "tragic troubadour" archetype—a traveling country performer who lives hard, dies prematurely, and continues singing to the bitter end.[13]

Hank Williams was the heir to Rodgers's place as country music's king as well as its most tragic troubador. Williams, whom I discuss in chapter 2, started life among the poorest of the poor in rural Alabama and moved while a boy to the city of Greenville, where he would learn music from African-American blues singer Rufus "Tee-Tot" Payne. Hank later launched his career from Montgomery and infused all the pathos, earthiness, and sensuality of the blues into country music. He took the music world by storm, but the tragic components of his personal life would conspire to end his life and career. He died in 1952 at age twenty-nine. Hank has become a country music deity. His music is seen almost as a platonic eternal form—the essence of what "real" or "pure" country music is. Thus, Moe Bandy could sing on behalf of country artists and fans, "Hank Williams, You Wrote My Life," while Waylon Jennings could protest changes in the country music industry in the 1970s by declaring, "I Don't Think Hank Done it This Way."

The question of authenticity arises frequently in country music. In 1975 Charlie Rich burned the envelope in protest of

---

[13] Ellison, *Country Music Culture*, 26–65.

John Denver being named CMA Artist of the Year. A year earlier, the Association of Country Entertainers was established in protest of Olivia Newton-John winning the Country Music Association's award for top female artist. To hear folks talk about what "they" were doing to "our" music, one would think the apocalypse was imminent. Ironically, the protesters were producing music that, with its silly orchestral and choral "Nashville Sound" background effects, often sounded more cosmopolitan and less "country" than the simpler arrangements and more traditional instrumentation of the "folkie" newcomers. The crossover trend reached its zenith with the 1980 film *Urban Cowboy*, as John Travolta taught the nation that country too could have a disco dance beat. In the wake of *Urban Cowboy*'s popularity, Barbara Mandrell declared her pride in being country "When Country Wasn't Cool," but by this time, most country artists had become country when country wasn't country.

From the ashes of post-disco country music arose a new traditionalist movement, spearheaded by George Strait. Strait's first single, "Unwound," a good ol' Texas-style honky-tonk celebration of lost love and cheap whiskey, bolted into the top ten and redirected the course of country music. Strait was a major influence on artists like Randy Travis, who revived working-class country music with his traditional themes and straightforward singing style, and Alan Jackson, who parodied the way the whole world has "Gone Country" in the 1990s. And, it was while listening to and being "blown away" by Strait's "Unwound" that one Troyal Garth Brooks decided to become a country star. Brooks has been criticized for not being "country" enough because his musical influences include arena rock bands like KISS and Queen and pop artists like Billy Joel, Don McLean, Dan

Fogleberg, and James Taylor. It could be said that in Brooks, all the chickens have come home to roost; country and rock, having both emerged from the ferment of white folks' cultural appropriation of the blues in the middle of the twentieth century, are rejoined at the turn of the millennium. Country music, then, covers a multitude of sins—or at least encompasses a multitude of musical styles, themes, and backgrounds. Part of my challenge in this book will be to argue convincingly that country music really is the music of a marginalized people, when, at the time of this writing, country enjoys the widest popularity of all American radio formats and appeals to the wealthiest and best-educated of radio audiences. Country music's domination of the music industry during the first three quarters of the 1990s testifies both that American culture is becoming more traditional and that country music culture has become more sophisticated.

This "mainstreamization" of country music, however, should not be seen as a linear progression. Richard Peterson has identified a "hard core/soft shell" dialectic in the history of country music: country music has alternated between stages of widely popular country-politan styles and more narrowly popular traditional "country" styles.[14] Early indications are that country's 1990s popularity boom has reached its peak and is beginning to wane. While interpreters like Cecilia Tichi emphasize country music's consistency with mainstream culture and its accessibility to

---

[14] Richard A. Peterson, *Creating Country Music: Fabricating Authenticity* (Chicago: University of Chicago Press, 1997); see also Richard A. Peterson, "The Dialectic of Hard-Core and Soft-Shell Country Music," *South Atlantic Quarterly* 94/1 (Spring 1995): 273–300; Richard A. Peterson and Roger Kern, "Hard-Core and Soft-Shell Country Fans," *Journal of Country Music* 17/1 (1995): 3–6.

(multi)cultural elites, the bulk of the scholarly literature on country music views country music primarily as the voice of the white working class. Bill Malone, the dean of country music historians, sees country music as primarily Southern and rural in origin and outlook.[15] Buffwack and Oermann, in their seminal—or should I say ovulal—work on women in country music, have shown that the deepest roots of country music's traditions lie in working-class women's musical practices.[16] Theologian and sociologist Tex Sample analyzes country music as, "White Soul," in that it embodies the lived values and contradictions of white working-class life.[17] In a more popular vein, journalist Lawrence Leamer points again and again to the music's poor white Southern rural roots in his excellent chronicle of country music in the 1990s.[18] Granted, as a commercial form and as a folk tradition, which even prior to its commercial emergence, had incorporated products of mass culture,[19] country music has never been completely isolated from the mainstream. But country music *is* legitimately read as the music of a people who *have* been separate from the mainstream. The redneck community

---

[15] Malone's *Country Music USA* (Austin: University of Texas Press, 1985) is the standard history of country music.

[16] Mary A. Bufwack and Robert K. Oermann, *Finding Her Voice: The Illustrated History of Women in Country Music* (New York: Henry Holt and Company, 1993).

[17] Tex Sample, *White Soul: Country Music, the Church, and Working Americans* (Nashville: Abingdon Press, 1996).

[18] Lawrence Leamer, *Three Chords and the Truth: Behind the Scenes with Those Who Make and Shape Country Music* (New York: HarperPaperbacks, 1997).

[19] See Malone, *Singing Cowboys*, 6–68.

constitutes country's hard core audience as identified in Peterson's dialectic.

Honky-Tonkology: How (Not) to Read Country Music

I mentioned above that I am not the first academic interpreter of country music to employ inaccurate or misleading terms for the sake of good-sounding titles. Cecelia Tichi's much heralded *High Lonesome: The American Culture of Country Music*[20] has been criticized by David Whisnant as a pretentious effort that fails on several counts: the first of which is its slightly misleading title.[21] Tichi's book is not about bluegrass music, which readers in the know would associate with the phrase "high lonesome," but about the way generic country music expresses the same generic American loneliness (and other generic themes) that the great American literary figures have expounded.

Tichi's other "major problems," according to Whisnant, include "thin scholarship" (Tichi consults only a small portion of the previous academic literature on country music.); generalizing that country music is "American" music in a broad sense (even if Chet Atkins did call it "our heritage"); and ignoring the subtle and not-so-subtle tensions and contradictions within country music, within American culture, and between country music and American culture (Are there really any generic Americans? Is there a generic

---

[20] Cecelia Tichi, *High Lonesome: The American Culture of Country Music* (Chapel Hill: University of North Carolina Press, 1994).

[21] David Whisnant, "Gone Country: *High Lonesome* and the Politics of Writing About Country Music," *Journal of Country Music* 17/2 (1995): 62–66.

American loneliness that could be shared by Hank Williams and Walt Whitman?). Whisnant's critique can be summarized in the following lyrics, sung to the tune of the Alan Jackson song from which Whisnant borrows his title, "Gone Country" (Bear in mind my opening comments about country's propensity toward slightly misleading descriptions—this time for the sake of rhyme):

> She was teaching in Nashville, writin' books about American lit,
> She noticed how those folks on music row kept making hit after hit
> She was tired of writin' books about Walt Whitman that no one was buyin'
> Thought she could write one about country music without hardly tryin'
> A few sweeping generalizations, and it didn't take long
> To prove that ol' Walt Whitman wrote country songs
>
> She's gone country, back to her books
> She's gone country, with a new way to look
> She's gone country, the academy's been took
> She's gone country—there she goes!

I agree with Whisnant that Tichi's book is highly problematic—and in may ways, I might add, downright silly. Ironically, in a follow-up piece—her editorial preface to a special theme issue of *South Atlantic Quarterly* titled *Readin' Country Music: Steel Guitars, Opry Stars and Honky Tonk Bars*—Tichi states her desire to combat the same types of

Introduction 17

problems Whisnant finds in her previous book. She describes her frustration with a session on country music at the Society for the Study of Narrative Literature, in which the panelists drew sweeping conclusions based on very shallow immersions into the music and its history and culture. She also acknowledges that country music cannot be "our" music in any broad sense, but that it is one of our musics and is therefore deserving of serious scholarly attention.[22]

But the same type of pretentiousness identified by Whisnant in her earlier book are again evident. First, there's the troubling assertion that "so little attention" has been given to country music, despite the fact that some of the contributors to her collection have been doing country music scholarship for nearly thirty years. Second, there's her stated "goal...that any reader's relation to country music change markedly," as if none of us had a healthy relationship to country music before being enlightened by Tichi and her assemblage. Third, she claims that the volume breaks new ground in the area of fair use with respect to copyrighted material, but most of the articles employ the tentative paraphrasing of songs to which readers of popular music scholarship are accustomed.

Once again, there's a pretentious title, seen in the dropping of the final "g" from readin'. Those persons who would pronounce their participles without a "g" would not consider country music to be something one would "read." Something to listen to, dance to, drink to, cry to, make love to, or maybe even preach against, but not something to read. Moreover, those who *would* see country music as something

---

[22] Tichi, "Editor's Note," *South Atlantic Quarterly* 94/1 (Spring 1995): 1–5.

to read would tend to look with derision upon those who habitually drop the "g" from their participles. The rhyming phrases in the subtitle add cuteness to the pretense. Perhaps the rhymes mask Tichi's secret ambition to be a country music songwriter rather than a mere interpreter, or perhaps the whole title should be blamed on Duke University Press's marketing gurus rather than on the editor.

Most of the selections in the issue are solid efforts by knowledgeable scholars producing valuable insights into country music and its culture. But in a few of the articles, including the more questionable ones, a common thread can be discerned that reveals the core problem with Tichi's approach to country music. For example, Teresa Ortega's piece on Johnny Cash as a lesbian icon is a personal experience narrative rather than a scholarly essay. The fact that this is the only non-scholarly selection raises the question of the reasons for its inclusion. My impression is that it is included—for the same reason as Tichi and Michael Kurek's piece on classical composer Paul Martin Zonn, Vivien Fryd's piece on painter Thomas Hart Benton, Pamela Wilson's analysis of Dolly Parton's image construction, Teresa Goddu's far-fetched attempt to trace the violence in Garth Brooks's videos to country's bluegrass roots and the link both to the social problem of violence against women, and perhaps even Mary Bufwack and Robert Oermann's reflection on their groundbreaking research into the roles of women in country music—to show that one can understand country music without bothering to try to understand rednecks. Country music is completely accessible to the highbrow (multi)cultural elite. It is a seedbed of covert feminism, an inspiration for lesbian iconography, a subject for high art, and a repository of melodies which can be woven into classical compositions.

Tichi acknowledges that the reluctance of scholars to take country music seriously stems from "it's association with a social sector that the intelligentsia has been reluctant, even loathe, to engage, namely, lower-class whites."[23] Her solution however, is not to challenge the intelligentsia to abandon their loathing, but to provide an access to country music that allows one to keep one's prejudices intact. Tichi fails to take seriously country music's social location; she fails to acknowledge country as the music of the redneck and the redneck as a member of a marginalized community. So rednecks remain the one group whom it's OK to loathe without jeopardizing one's perceived political correctness.

I do not contend that projects such as examining the latent feminism in country music are invalid—I will attempt as much later in this book. My contention, in fact, is that country music is at its core the music of a marginalized group—the rednecks. In his book *White Soul: Country Music, the Church and the Working American*, Tex Sample analyzes country music as a window through which mainline Protestant churches can come to understand the white working class. My approach is, in a sense, the inverse of Sample's. I keep in view country's mostly Southern rural and working class social context in order to understand the music's theological meanings.

---

[23] Ibid., 3.

My Own Voice

I cannot claim that I grew up on a farm or in a holler or that my family used to gather round the radio to listen to broadcasts of the Opry when I was a child. The truth is that I grew up in the suburbs of a medium-sized southern city, in a relatively affluent family. I started listening to country music when I was a teenager—partly because I was learning to play guitar and country songs were easy to learn and play—but mostly because I was attracted to the ethos of country music: the sense of humor and irony in the face of life's troubles. When I tell my wife Malinda that listening to country music is researching the folk traditions of my people, she reminds me: "You don't have any people!" So who am I to claim to write authentically on behalf of rural working-class southerners?

My interest in trying to relate theological scholarship to working-class reality was born before I returned to school to pursue a Ph.D. in Christian Ethics, when I was serving as pastor of a congregation in a rural Carolina textile-mill community. For a little over three years, I spent my time walking alongside people who struggled daily to figure out what it means to serve Jesus while also struggling to make a living in this world and deal with the grief and loss life inevitably brings. These three years spent visiting in their homes, walking with them through the halls of hospitals and mortuaries, and audaciously presuming to try to preach the gospel among them week in and week out comprised the most valuable years of my education, ironically the only three of my first thirty-six years during which I was not enrolled in some educational institution. One thing, at least, was clear: the literature published by Christian publishers did not seem to address the reality of the folks among whom I was ministering. Further, it did not seem to be interested in addressing their reality. I cannot promise that this book will be particularly helpful to rural pastors. But I do think country music can serve as a window to the working-class worldview. I also think that country music sometimes expresses truths as profound as those found in the theological tomes to which professors and their students usually devote their attention.

As I've presented and listened to papers at scholarly meetings related to the themes in this book, one issue has often arisen in the ensuing discussions. My work—and the work of most interpreters of country music—is heavily focused on the interpretation of country music lyrics. Certainly, musicologists suggest, there is something to be said about the music. Well, perhaps there is. But country music is more lyric-driven than most other musical genres. In fact, one explanation sometimes suggested for country music's recent popularity surge is that aging baby boomers want music in which they can understand the words. Legendary country songwriter Harlan Howard, when asked what makes a good country song, replied "three chords and the truth." Generally speaking, it's always the same three chords: the one, four, five progression.[24] As Kinky Friedman wryly observes, "I love all of Tom T. Hall's songs and both of his melodies."[25] So it's the *truth*, rather than the three chords, that deserves most of the attention. I will comment

---

[24] The one-four-five chord progression also constitutes the basic structure of blues and classic rock and roll—testimony to country and rock's shared ancestry. I'll leave it to the musicologists to argue the significance of the chord progression itself.
[25] Kinky Friedman, *Road Kill* (New York: Simon & Schuster, 1997) 236.

from time to time on features of the musical performance in the songs I discuss, but my focus will be on the lyrics and the meanings they convey.

So if you'll read along with me through the next few chapters, I'll do my best to see that you are informed about the history of country music, the worlds of meaning it constructs, the values it embodies, and the people for whom it speaks. And I'll try to keep you entertained in the process.

1

The Gospel Songs and the Cheatin' Songs:

Suffering and the Failure of Redneck Theology

Cheatin' songs. That's real poor man music. Rich guys don't even understand somebody like Hank Williams. A rich man hardly needs a woman at all. If she runs away, who cares? he'll go get another one. But when you've got nothing and not much to look forward to, then if your woman runs off and you lose the one good thing in your life, man, that just about kills you.... It's like they say, a song only gives you a taste of what you already know. We

> oughta get out of gospel and into cheatin' songs, cause that's what we know.[1]
> —Fictional gospel singer Wendell Shepherd in Garrison Keillor's *WLT: A Radio Romance*

> People who have not been oppressed physically cannot know the power inherent in bodily expressions of love.... In a world where a people possess little that is their own, human relationships are placed at a premium. The love between men and women becomes immediate and real.[2]
> —James Cone in *The Spirituals and the Blues*

"A song only gives you a taste of what you already know," declares Garrison Keillor's fictional gospel crooner Wendell Shepherd. What Wendell already knows, and presumes that his audience knows even better, is the experience of suffering. Country music, whether sacred or secular, is a music of and for people acquainted with sorrow. Hazel Dickens captured this basic truth about country music when she borrowed Pete Seeger's phrase *Hard Hitting Songs for Hard Hit People* as the title of one of her country albums in the 1980s. Keith Whitley, whose life and death evoke the lyrics of a sad country song, expressed the situation of anyone who really appreciates country music in his anthem, "I'm No Stranger to the Rain." Gospel songs and cheatin' songs are suffering songs.

---

[1] Garrison Keillor, *WLT: A Radio Romance* (New York: Viking, 1991) 350–51.

[2] James Cone, *The Spirituals and the Blues* (Maryknoll NY: Orbis, 1992) 114–15.

The Gospel Songs and the Cheatin' Songs 25

Gospel songs and cheatin' songs are also questioning songs. The opening lines of the old gospel hymn "Farther Along" ask plaintively: "Tempted and tried we're oft made to wonder/ Why it should be thus all the day long/ While there are others living about us/ Never molested though in the wrong." This song cuts directly to the chase, raising the basic existential question of theodicy: Why do the innocent suffer while the wicked prosper? Cheatin' songs similarly raise questions regarding the structures of moral meaning. John Anderson sings of being bothered by doubts about his lover's fidelity because "She Just Started Liking Cheating Songs," and he's not sure whether her attraction is to the cheating or to the melody. Here a moral order that previously had been taken for granted is called into question. The questioning nature of cheatin' songs is expressed in Juice Newton's "Who's Cheatin' Who?" recently covered by Alan Jackson: "Who's cheatin' who, who's being used, and who don't even care anymore?" In cheatin' songs, the moral structures that are supposed to give meaning, order, and fulfillment—typically the structures of marital commitment and fidelity—become a source of frustration, repression, confusion, and anxiety.

Gospel songs and cheatin' songs function for the redneck community in ways analogous to the ways the spirituals and the blues have functioned for the slave communities and their descendants. Like the spirituals and the blues, they express an awareness that something is out of kilter with the moral structure(s) of the universe. James Cone, Jon Michael Spencer, Anthony Pinn, and other African-American theologians have argued that spirituals, blues, and other African-American musical traditions represent theological explorations and that the question at the root of all

African-American theology is the question of theodicy: How could a just God allow unjust suffering to prevail in the world? Gospel songs and cheatin' songs similarly struggle with basic existential questions, especially the question of theodicy. They are primary theological texts—efforts to make sense of raw experience by (de)constructing systems of meaning and order. They are texts of theological *liberation* because they respond to experiences of oppression and marginalization.

Southern Gospel: How Southern? How Gospel?

When I speak of "gospel songs," I have in mind the world of Southern gospel music[3]—the music associated with all-day singing and dinner on the grounds. This is the world of quartets whose tenors vie to see who can sing the highest while the basses vie to see who can sing the lowest. It is sometimes portrayed as a world of pastel polyester suits and big hair—a world that exudes and in some ways creates the kind of "tacky" taste enshrined in Elvis Presley's Graceland estate. In fact, Elvis himself aspired to be a Southern gospel quartet member, but failed his audition with gospel promoter Eldridge Fox. According to Fox, despite the vocal capabilities

---

[3] For a comprehensive history of Southern Gospel Music, see James R. Goff, *Close Harmony: A History of Southern Gospel* (Chapel Hill: University of North Carolina Press, 2002). My account is drawn primarily from Don Cusic, *The Sound of Light: A History of Gospel Music* (Bowling Green OH: Bowling Green State University Popular Press, 1990). For interpretation of Southern Gospel Music, see Michael Graves and David Fillingim, eds., *More than "Precious Memories": The Rhetoric of Southern Gospel Music* (Macon: Mercer University Press, 2004).

The Gospel Songs and the Cheatin' Songs   27

and showmanship that would make him the King, Elvis lacked the ear for harmony necessary for blending in with a quartet. Elvis did record a number of gospel songs and had the Southern Gospel quartet J. D. Sumner and the Stamps tour with him to sing backup. The culture of Southern gospel music has evolved from the ethos and pathos of the frontier camp-meeting, the nineteenth-century revivalist theology of Dwight Moody and his hymn-writing song-leader Ira Sankey, and the revival showmanship of their successors Billy Sunday and his song-leader Homer Rodeheaver.

More specifically, the musical form known as Southern Gospel music originated as a promotional strategy by publishing houses to sell sheet music. The publishers would sponsor annual "singing schools" at various locations. Quartets would travel to these singing schools and perform the latest available pieces. The music caught on (i.e., was appropriated by the "folk") and has evolved into a large industry. Southern Gospel, however, has remained farther from the American cultural mainstream than country music. A newer phenomenon, known as Christian Country Music, emerged during the 1990s as the "sacred" analog to hot, new, suburban, secular country, leaving traditional Southern Gospel with its mostly rural and working-class audience intact. The culture of Southern Gospel revolves around huge annual events like the week-long National Quartet Convention (which recently moved from Nashville to Louisville in part to get out of country music's hegemonic shadow), annual all-night gospel sings in such places as

Waycross, Georgia;[4] Bonifay, Florida; and thousands of smaller sings at gospel music parks, camp-meetings, and churches. There are certainly grounds for questioning the gospel song tradition's authenticity as a reflection of the redneck community. The gospel hymns of the Moody-Sankey era, precursors to contemporary gospel songs, were composed almost exclusively by Northerners.[5] The forms of organized religion in the South were shaped by denominational bodies from the North. As the Civil War approached and denominations began to split, the Southern denominational organizations became handmaidens of the white Southern oligarchy. A pure grassroots redneck religion is hard to find. Even today, working class religion is heavily influenced by outside ideological forces through the "professional evangelicalism" of the religious right.[6] Yet "a basic and honest faith," which has "survive[d] major theological movements as if they had never existed," persists among redneck people.[7]

Redneck faith persists in the face of extreme suffering. My experience as a rural Southern preacher indicates, and a

---

[4] See David Fillingim, "Music Stretching to the Heavens," *Seabreeze: The Guide to Coastal Living* 1 (September/October 1986): 20–21.

[5] Sandra Sizer, *Gospel Hymns and Social Religion: The Rhetoric of Nineteenth-Century Revivalism* (Philadelphia: Temple University Press, 1978) 23.

[6] Darren Cushman-Wood, "Redneck Liberation Theology: Recovering a Radical Gospel for White, Working-Class Evangelicals," *The Other Side* 28 (October 1992): 46–49.

[7] Will Campbell, "The World of the Redneck," *Katallagate: Journal of the Committee of Southern Churchmen* 5 (Spring).

stroll through any church graveyard in the rural South will confirm, that so-called "Appalachian dead-baby songs" are not "gothic," as has recently been suggested;[8] rather, they provide painful portraits of the real-life experience of rural families. The infant mortality rate in rural America has consistently been higher than the overall national rate, and the rural South scores worse than other regions on low birth weight and a host of other public health measures.[9] The redneck community is no stranger to suffering and tragedy. Rural working-class folks, who have often struggled just to meet basic needs, are not subject to the illusion that life should be free of problems. Yet it is because of the prominence of the religious faith of these folks that the region has come to be called the "Bible Belt."

Sandra Sizer has delineated a two-part rhetorical strategy by which the nineteenth-century Moody-Sankey gospel hymns—especially hymns about heaven—respond to the conditions of life in this world. First, they look forward to heaven as the perfect antithesis to earthly suffering. Second, they look inward, defining faith in terms of affections or individual psychodynamics, removing the external conditions of earthly life from religious relevance. The appropriate

---

[8] Teresa Goddu, "Bloody Daggers and Lonesome Graveyards: The Gothic and Country Music," *South Atlantic Quarterly* 94/1 (Winter 1995): 57–80.

[9] Leslie L. Clarke and Michael K. Miller, "The Character and Prospects of Rural Community Health and Medical Care," in *American Rural Communities*, edited by A. E. Luloff and Louis E. Swanson (Boulder: Westview Press, 1990); Louis E. Swanson, "The Human Dimension of the Rural South in Crisis," in *The Rural South in Crisis: Challenges for the Future*, edited by Lionel J. Beaulieu (Boulder: Westview Press, 1988).

response to suffering, according to the gospel song tradition, is not to do battle with unjust or oppressive social structures, but to wait patiently and passively for future rewards while trusting Jesus to calm one's inner tensions in the meantime.[10] The most popular Southern Gospel songs are those about heaven. These songs respond to the conditions of life in this world following the same strategy identified by Sizer in the earlier gospel song tradition.

As the hymn advises, "Cheer up, my brother, live in the sunshine; we'll understand it all by and by." Contemporary gospel songs, like earlier camp-meeting hymns, advocate the utter rejection of life in this world.[11] This world has no value; therefore, worldly suffering is not to be taken seriously. In "Leavin' on My Mind," for example, Rusty Goodman describes the deteriorating condition of his earthly home, then denies that any effort to make repairs would be worthwhile because of his urgent desire to depart from this world. The same dichotomy between a decrepit earthly dwelling and a glorious heavenly home is also expressed in "Mansion Over the Hilltop" and "Wait'll You See My Brand New Home." The contrast between the pain experienced in this life and the perfect bliss of heaven is a repeated theme. Songs such as "Looking for a City" and "Tears will Never Stain the Streets of that City" contrast the countless tears cried on earth with the absence of grief in heaven. "Hallelujah Square" promises a joyous reunion with lost loved ones that will put an end to the bitter grief of separation and loss. "Your Ride's on the

---

[10] Sizer *Gospel Hymns and Social Religion*, 31–35.

[11] See Dickson Bruce, *And They All Sang Hallelujah: Plain-Folk Camp-Meeting Religion, 1800–1845* (Knoxville: University of Tennessee Press, 1974) 96–105.

Way" posits the joy of heaven as compensation for the suffering that comes with disease. "Sweet Beulah Land" expresses a mournful homesickness for heaven as the bittersweet condition in which earthbound Christians find themselves. Other songs posit the anticipation of heaven as a source of joy during earthly life: up-tempo numbers such as "Touring that City," "Canaanland is Just in Sight," "City of Gold," and "I Feel Like Travelin' On" are toe-tapping celebrations of good things to come.

All in all, the gospel songs acknowledge that life is filled with misery, but suffering is not to be resisted. Suffering is to be borne patiently, with the confidence that a better home lies beyond the horizon. Present suffering will be compensated "by and by." Even those songs that do not directly emphasize heaven as the remedy to all suffering treat human misery lightly. "Just a little talk with Jesus" is all that is needed. One does not resist suffering; one merely adjusts one's attitude toward suffering through proper religious affections.

The gospel songs recognize the reality of the experience of suffering, but not its legitimacy. Suffering is an unfortunate and unavoidable coincidence of being human, but one the Christian should rise above through faith. Thus the gospel songs, unlike the slave spirituals, have functioned to prevent conscientization[12] and liberative praxis. The spirituals exude an ambiguity in which, for example, crossing over Jordan into the promised land refers to both crossing the river

---

[12] *Conscientization* is a term coined by Brazilian educator and theorist Paulo Freire and used widely among liberation theologians and Christian peace and justice activists to refer to the consciousness-raising that occurs as a first step in participating in liberation movements. See Mary Elizabeth Mullino Moore, *Teaching From the Heart: Theology and Educational Method* (Minneapolis: Fortress Press, 1991) 166-71.

of death into heaven and crossing the Ohio River into the free states.[13] The spirituals, therefore, embody a conviction that God intends to move history on earth toward justice, thus providing a foundation for liberative praxis that the white gospel songs lack. The gospel songs' strategies of postponement and internalization posit an ultimate discontinuity between earthly life and just rewards. The bridge of death must be crossed before one receives the rewards for righteousness; therefore, conditions of earthly injustice are beyond religious concern. The absolute individualism that results from the gospel songs' internalization of religious faith also mitigates against liberation. Each *individual* soul will be judged; therefore, the collective action and community solidarity required in the struggle for social justice are beyond the pale of religious faith.

The African-American musical traditions, then, are characterized by an ambiguity, a commingling, in which body and spirit move together. One looks forward both to the ultimate bliss of heaven and to all the penultimate goods that come when social structures are brought into closer conformity with biblical standards of equality and justice. One engages in the struggle for justice as a primary expression of one's faithfulness to the God who frees slaves and the Christ who by his resurrection overcomes oppression at the hands of unjust rulers. The faith expressed in these songs, to use a theological term, is incarnational. God's intentions for human beings find full expression in embodied earthly life. In contrast, the white gospel song tradition is simply dualistic. Body and spirit are separate entities with separate destinies. The only purpose of embodied earthly life

---

[13] Cone, *The Spirituals and the Blues*, 81.

is to determine one's eternal destiny. Eternity in heaven, not time on earth, is the sole purpose of life.

A Brief History of the Cheatin' Song

Since the historical roots of modern country music are complex and difficult to trace, the roots of cheatin' songs as a specific form will also be difficult to discern. Faithless love was among the themes of the eighteenth and nineteenth century English ballads often considered to be the most influential of modern country music's historical antecedents. The Carter family's first recording, "Bury Me Beneath the Willow," a typical "Celtic" or "hillbilly" ballad, tells the story of a man whose lover proved unfaithful. However, in the traditional ballads, transgressing conventional sexual norms is looked upon negatively and often associated with death—specifically the murder of the sexually active female.[14] These songs served as a form of social control, encouraging listeners—especially women—to remain within the safe confines of Victorian sexual norms. Cheatin' songs, on the other hand, often accept sexual unfaithfulness as a necessary and even celebrated part of living.

The early hillbilly recordings, with their traditional approach to love and sex, reinforced an image of the mountaineer as morally and culturally superior to the burgeoning urban industrial chaos.[15] It was not long, however, before the hillbilly was included in the long-standing stereotype

---

[14] See Roger D. Abrahams and George Foss, *Anglo-American Folksong Style* (Englewood Cliffs NJ: Prentice-Hall, 1968) chapter 6.

[15] See Bill Malone, *Singing Cowboys and Musical Mountaineers: Southern Culture and the Roots of Country Music* (Athens: University of Georgia Press, 1993) 80–81.

of rural Southerners as ignorant, impulsive, irrational dupes.[16] The growth of the negative hillbilly stereotype may be one factor contributing to the rise of the cowboy as the dominant image for country musicians. Cheatin' songs belong to the subgenre of country music known as "honky-tonk" music. The honky-tonk movement took off with the repeal of prohibition, which happened to coincide with the rapid industrialization and urbanization of the South and the increased transition from farming to other types and locales of work. The oilfields and refineries of Texas became the center of the honky-tonk craze, with Texas troubador Ernest Tubb becoming its biggest and brightest star. Honky-tonk music featured a loud, raucous performance style (necessary to be heard over the din of a crowded, smoke-filled bar) often with a walking bass line and a rhythm for dancing. The subject matter of honky-tonk songs includes lost love, illicit love, and drinking.

Hank Williams's music clearly shows the influence of honky-tonk tradition in both style and content. Hank's singing style shows an explicit effort to emulate Tubb, along with the more mournful but sedate influence of Roy Acuff, the king of the hillbilly singers, and the blues inflections of Rodgers and especially "Tee-Tot" Payne, the African-American street-singer who was Hank's first music teacher. Honky-tonk culture is a response to the desperation of working-class life. As noted in the quotes by Cone and Keillor at the head of this chapter, economic deprivation

---

[16] Ibid., 90; see also "When Whites Migrate from the South," *US News & World Report* 55 (14 October 1963): 70–73; George Tindal, "The Benighted South: Origins of a Modern Image," *Virginia Quarterly Review* 40 (Spring 1964): 281–94.

raises the stakes of romance to the level of ultimate concern. Yet an encounter with the ultimate carries with it the potential either to redeem or to destroy. Honky-tonk music—cheatin' and drinkin' songs—seeks to ameliorate the destructive power of romantic love. As Tubb sings: "May baby's gone, gone, gone,/ And I'm alone—so, so alone;/ And I've got nothing else to lose/ So bartender, pass the booze."

Floyd Tillman's 1949 hit "Slipping Around" is perhaps the first widely successful cheatin' song. But it was Hank's career, a watershed for country music in general, that made cheatin' songs a way of life. Cheatin' songs have had a consistent presence in country music despite the repeated efforts to make the music more sophisticated and mainstream. In the 1970s and early 1980s, amidst the crossover fever accompanying the post-disco "Urban Cowboy" phenomenon, Moe Bandy helped to ward off the death of "real" country music with his many cheatin' and drinkin' songs.[17] *Billboard* magazine's November 1994 One-Hundreth Anniversary edition named "Walk on By," a cheatin' song written by Kendall Hayes, as the number one country music record of all time. Cheatin' songs have continued to constitute a significant portion of the repertoires of country musicians.

Justice, Redemption, and the Body

Cheatin' songs, like gospel songs, represent responses to the experience of suffering in the world. Some cheatin' songs effect a sensualization of the eschatology of the gospel songs.

---

[17] Bill Malone, "Honky Tonk: The Music of the Southern Working Class," in *Folk Music and Modern Sound*, edited by William Ferris and Mary L. Hart (Jackson: University Press of Mississippi, 1982) 127.

Mark Chesnutt's "Broken-Promise Land," into which the cheaters are about to enter, alludes to the gospel song tradition's tendency to spiritualize the biblical exodus story as a metaphor for entering heaven. The Kendalls reject gospel music's version of heaven in their hit, "Heaven's Just a Sin Away" (which was answered by a gospel song to the same tune titled "Heaven's Just a Prayer Away"). In cheatin' songs, bodily resolution of existential tension becomes a vehicle of redemption. The cheatin' songs thus share with the blues the rejection of body/spirit dualism.[18] The cheatin' songs are in effect the redneck blues—the music of an oppressed people seeking to transcend but not ignore their experience. Cone's analysis of the blues, quoted at the head of this chapter, is instructive on the functional similarity between blues and cheatin' songs. First, the experience of oppression awakens an awareness of the sacredness of the body: "People who have not been oppressed physically cannot know the power inherent in bodily expressions of love." Moreover, economic disadvantage heightens the significance of love relationships: "In a world where a people possess little that is their own, human relationships are placed premium. The love between men and women becomes immediate and real."

Cheatin' songs, like the blues, refuse to look forward or inward in an effort to deny cruel realities or to postpone the hope of redemption. They seek instead an immediate resolution and response to the pain of bodily existence. Cheatin' songs and blues reject otherworldly dualism in favor of bodily acts of protest against the contradictions of life at the social margins. The honky-tonk movement was fueled in large part by the rural Southerner's pilgrimage from the farm to the urban factory.

---

[18] See Cone, *The Spirituals and the Blues*, 114–18.

While John Greenway groups "the strong rhythms of country-western music" with "sex and liquor" as things that are naturally appealing to "the human organism,"[19] sex carries a capacity for deep personal and spiritual transformation that the other two lack.[20]

Some cheatin' songs do maintain the notion that cheating is morally inappropriate and insist that some type of basic justice for the wrongdoers is inevitable. Hank Williams posits the inevitable payback when he sings, "Your cheatin' heart, will tell on you." Similarly, Willie Nelson conjectures that his unfaithful partner's comeuppance is only a matter of time in "Funny How Time Slips Away." Kenny Rogers's "Ruby Don't Take Your Love to Town" (written by Mel Tillis) and Garth Brooks's "Papa Loved Mama" portray the type of sexual revenge that Susan Jacoby calls "wild justice."[21]

Ironically, when women sing of justice for cheating, it is generally the other woman who is called to task and not the offending man. Loretta Lynn threatens her female competitor in "Fist City." In "Nobody," Sylvia expresses her suspicions arising from unexplained anonymous phone calls and then promises to exact revenge on the other woman by out-loving her. Reba McEntire will outdo "Whoever's in New England" with patience, promising to let bygones be bygones when her lover's paramour is finished with him. Tammy Wynette, of course, advises "Stand By Your Man," no matter what.

---

[19] John Greenway, *"Country-Western: The Music of America," The American West* 5 (November 1968): 33.

[20] See Wendell Berry, *Sex, Economy, Freedom & Community* (New York: Pantheon, 1992) 117ff.

[21] Susan Jacoby, *Wild Justice: The Evolution of Revenge* (New York: Harper & Row, 1983).

Underlying this apparent feminine passivity is what I call a honky-tonk feminist critique of patriarchy. The assumption is that men are simply incapable of moral agency; therefore, it's up to women to uphold the moral order. ("After all, he's just a man," sings Wynette.) The general absence of accusations against men in the cheatin' songs is somewhat analogous to the absence of indictments of white owners in the slave spirituals. From the perspective of the oppressed group, the mistreatment of African peoples through slavery proved that white people had no consciences—white people apparently were not human, so there was no point in trying to hold whites to standards of human decency or human ethics.[22] Similarly, in women's country music, the oppression of women by men is evidence that men lack the capacity for moral agency.

The idea that women are solely responsible for the state of the world's morality finds some reinforcement songs by male country singers. Gary Stewart laments, "She's Actin' Single (I'm Drinkin' Doubles)," while Sonny Curtis pontificates "Good ol' boys will be good ol' boys until the good ol' girls go bad." Such songs tell of the catastrophic results of women's abandoning their role as guardians of the moral order. Of course, the stereotypical songs celebrating male rowdiness testify to men's moral ineptitude.

There is, however, at least one significant direct indictment of men. Kitty Wells's classic, "It Wasn't God Who Made Honky Tonk Angels," places the blame for cheating squarely on the shoulders of the male offenders, giving a direct answer to the theological question about suffering raised in the gospel songs. The song is also an answer, directly,

---

[22] Cone, *The Spirituals and the Blues*, 76.

to Hank Thompson's "The Wild Side of Life" and, by implication, to all other ways in which redneck culture places undue responsibility on women. The tendency in country music to place all responsibility for virtue on women is at least as old as the nineteenth-century murder ballads, in which a young woman is usually killed by her lover for no clear reason, but perhaps for simply failing to uphold her virtue.[23] Any remorse expressed by the perpetrators in these songs results from receiving punishment from the law rather than from any conviction that the act itself was wrong. Likewise, the men in cheatin' songs generally express regret only after losing the women they cheated on, cheated with, or both. But Wells answers that the blame for earthly suffering belongs neither to God nor to women, but to those who wield earthly power—men. Unfortunately, Wells offers no solution to the problem, and the solution offered by others is equally as passive as that of the gospel songs. Since only women have consciences, they are simply to put up with men. Yet women are to hold one another accountable in the meantime.

Other cheatin' songs offer a more radical protest, denying the relevance of justice by questioning the moral order itself. Care is taken to absolve the parties involved of moral responsibility. One approach is a fatalism, which interprets cheating as the inevitable response to a situation fraught with conflict and frustration. In "It's a Cheatin' Situation," Moe Bandy and Janie Fricke sing of cheating as something they "*have* to do"—the only possible response to loveless marriages. Other songs deconstruct the alleged moral

---

[23] See Kenneth D. Tunnell, "Blood Marks the Spot Where Poor Ellen Was Found: Violent Crime in Bluegrass Music," *Popular Music and Society* 15 (Fall 1991): 95–115.

order by promoting a simple subjectivism ("It Don't Feel Like Sinnin' to Me") or a moral nihilism (the devil-may care attitude toward right and wrong expressed in "Help Me Make it through the Night"). The cheatin' songs, then, like the blues, represent a survival strategy[24]—an effort to come to terms with the contradictions of following the rules as defined by society while being denied a proportional share of the goods of the society and with the sense of powerlessness which results from living in the midst of such contradictions.

The Failure of Redneck Theology

Gospel songs and cheatin' songs represent different types of theological responses to the problem of suffering. Gospel songs, unfortunately, have too often served as the tools of outside forces that sought to keep the redneck under control. By teaching Christians to endure patiently any and all suffering, gospel songs function to reinforce the status quo through an ideology of domesticity. This religious sanctioning of the status quo, coupled with the exploitation by political elites of the redneck's fear and hatred of black males, has contributed to the social conservatism of the redneck.[25] The working class appropriation of these songs as their own confirms Don Cusic's observation that one of the basic functions of music in American Christianity is as "a psychological sedative the church uses against the chaos and confusion of the secular world."[26]

---

[24] Cone, *The Spirituals and the Blues*, 119.
[25] See Campbell, "The World of the Redneck."
[26] Cusic, *The Sound of Light*, ii.

Cheatin' songs embody a greater sense of protest amidst conditions of perceived powerlessness. Yet, while sharing some of the sense of irony inherent in the blues, cheatin' songs tend to evoke a fatalism resembling that of the gospel songs. The blues "express a belief that one day things will not be like what they are today."[27] Cheatin' songs come closer to embodying the benediction Hank Williams often pronounced at the end of his concerts: "don't worry about nothin', cause it ain't gonna be alright nohow."[28]

Tex Sample has correctly noted that country music embodies a form of protest against the contradictions of working-class life. In the joyful abandon and moral defiance of the honky-tonk, and in the cheatin' songs' sense of irony about love, country music takes a stance of resistance against a dominant socioeconomic and moral/cultural order that dehumanizes working people. But it is a resistance of escape rather than engagement. If all suffering is simply unavoidable, then resignation and escape are the appropriate responses. But if at least some of the suffering that results from unjust social structures can be prevented, a stance of engagement in the struggle for justice is a better response. In other words, escapism may be an appropriate response to suffering, but if escapism is the first response, it precludes the possibility of social change. If redneck theology is to become redneck liberation theology, then, a primary task will be developing a perspective that assesses suffering critically,

---

[27] Cone, *The Spirituals and the Blues*, 124.

[28] Reported in Kent Blaser, "'Pictures from Life's Other Side': Hank Williams, Country Music, and Popular Culture in America," *South Atlantic Quarterly* 84 (1985): 12–26.

avoiding the fatalistic extremes of "How Beautiful Heaven Must Be" and "Welcome to Earth, Third Rock from the Sun."
So we must look more deeply into country music's traditions and examine more closely the varieties of country music's implicit theologies. When seeking to understand country music, it is proper first to consider Hank Williams, so it is to Hank that we turn next. Hank represents country music in its purest expression in part because he stands on both sides of the major tensions in country music: commercial vs. folk, marginal vs. mainstream, sacred vs. secular. In Hank's life and work, we will find a secularization of the hopeful longing we have seen in the gospel songs, but also a sacralization of the pessimism we have associated in this chapter with cheatin' songs. We will also discover in Hank Williams most of the standards by which all subsequent country music is judged.

2

The Gospel According to Hank:

Country Music's Hillbilly Humanist Moral Core

If you want to know country music just listen to a Hank Williams record.[1]
—country music historian Don Cusic

Moe Bandy (who happens to be a distant cousin of mine) sums up the place of Hank Williams in country music culture in the title of his hit song, "Hank Williams, You Wrote My Life." No artist embodies as much of what is meant by the designation "country music" as Hank. Hank's music manifests a mixture of rawness, simplicity, irony, and emotional depth

---

[1] Don Cusic, "Hear That Lonesome Whippoorwill: Hank Williams as Poet," in *Hank Williams: The Complete Lyrics,* edited by Don Cusic (New York: St. Martins, 1993) vii.

that makes it archetypal: all good country music exhibits these characteristics found in Hank's music, but no other artist exhibits these characteristics in their full perfection. In the country music pantheon, Hank sits in the place of highest honor. Hank's life, short but brilliant career, and death have become myth—even generating accounts of posthumous appearances to would-be disciples. Hank Williams wrote and sang the lives of country music listeners in a way that rang truer than in the work of any artist before or since.

Hank may have written our lives, but he lived *his* life—a brief, tragic, sometimes exhilarating but often lonely life. Hank's life and the longings expressed in his music reveal deep contradictions—contradictions that perhaps account for his wide appeal and his canonization by country music listeners. In this chapter, we will explore how the work of Hank Williams develops and expresses the core moral/theological outlook of country music.

The Life and Times of Hank Williams

King Hiram Williams was born 17 September 1923, in Mount Olive, Alabama, to the type of family for whom the designation "White Trash" was invented. Chet Flippo's account[2] of Hank's early years reads like a Flannery O'Connor story minus the happy ending. Hank lived the migratory life of the rural poor for most of his childhood. He was born with spina bifida occulta, a protrusion at the base of

---

[2] Chet Flippo, *Your Cheatin' Heart: A Biography of Hank Williams* (New York: St. Martin's, 1981). Other noteworthy biographies of Hank Williams are Roger Williams, *Sing a Sad Song: The Life of Hank Williams* (Champaign: University of Illinois Press, 1981) and Colin Escott, *Hank Williams: The Biography* (New York: Little, Brown & Company, 1995).

his spine that was never treated and that contributed to the quest for pharmaceutical pain relief that eventually killed him. His Father, Lon Williams, effectively vanished from Hank's life in 1930, checking into a V. A. hospital for chronic alcoholism.

Domineering is too pale a description for Hank's mother, Lilly Williams. After the departure of her husband, she moved her family (Hank and his older sister Irene) to Greenville, Alabama, where her primary source of income was running boardinghouses. She had Hank shine shoes and sell peanuts to supplement the family income. In Greenville, Hank had his first music teacher—an African-American street singer named Rufus "Tee-Tot" Payne. In 1937, the family moved to Montgomery. Hank, who had taken up street performing while still living in Greenville, soon entered an amateur night contest in Montgomery and win first prize by singing "W. P. A. Blues," a song he never recorded but that is believed to be the first song he wrote. This success led to a radio show in Montgomery, and Hank's career was underway.

Lilly took an active role in Hank's professional development, managing his schedule and his earnings. She regularly took Hank to the Baptist church, where she was organist, when he was a small child. But she apparently held a utilitarian assessment of religion, for when the world of the honky-tonks seemed to offer the best possible road to riches, Lilly Williams was ready to help her son down that road. Hank is reported to have complimented her suitability to the rough life of the honky-tonk circuit: "There ain't nobody in this here world I'd rather have standin' next to me in a beer joint brawl than my Maw with a broken bottle in her hand."[3]

When he was eighteen, Hank met and married (illegally—her divorce had been final for only ten days of the mandatory thirty-day waiting period) Audrey Sheppard. Their passionate and stormy relationship was riddled with fighting and making up, an annulment followed by an annulment of the annulment, and finally—after eight years together—a divorce. "Miss Audrey" took over many of the managerial duties from Lilly, and aspired to a singing career herself, despite a lack of recognizable talent. Hank and Audrey went to Nashville in September 1946 to see music publisher Fred Rose. According to legend, Rose challenged Hank to prove his songwriting ability by writing a song on the spot, and Hank responded by going into the next room and writing "Mansion on the Hill." Rose would become not only Hank's publisher and producer, but a friend, father figure, and collaborator. (The degree to which Rose "polished" Hank's rough compositions is a matter of heated debate among country music historians.)

Hank's first recordings for Sterling records in Nashville were moderately successful in 1946, leading to a recording contract with MGM in 1947. In his first MGM session, he recorded "Move It on Over," a rockabilly precursor that would become his first hit. He and his band, the Drifting Cowboys, moved from Montgomery to Shreveport to join the Louisiana Hayride, a sort of minor league version of Nashville's Grand Ole Opry. The year 1949 saw several major turning points for Hank. Foremost among these was the birth in May of his son, Randall Hank, called "Bocephus" by

---

[3] Flippo, *Your Cheatin' Heart,* 38.

his father but known to the rest of the world as Hank Jr. That year also brought Hank's first number one hit, a cover of the pop standard "Lovesick Blues," which led to an electrifying June guest appearance at the Opry. Hank's reception by the Opry audience and his persistent success on the charts meant that the Opry's management could no longer delay inviting him to become a regular member, despite wariness about his reputed drinking binges, violent outbursts, and general unpredictability.

Hank managed to stay relatively straight and sober for a while at the beginning of his Opry tenure, motivated in part by his desire to be a good family man. But the move to Nashville brought new pressures. The pressure of success, of balancing his vast popularity and new economic class status with his sense of who he was, weighed heavily upon him. His relationship with Audrey grew more tense and combative. His touring schedule was excruciating, and a musician's life on the road brings temptations all its own. Hank's drinking grew worse. By August 1952, just three years after Hank's glorious Opry debut and three months after his divorce from Audrey, Opry management had grown so disgruntled that they fired Hank.

Hank returned to the Louisiana Hayride, encouraged by Rose, who hoped Hank would clean up his act and soon return to Nashville. But, with his pride wounded by his banishment from country music's mother church and his heart broken at the loss of his family, Hank found more reasons to seek escape from his from demons. Soon, if not already, he was addicted not only to alcohol, but also to pills given to him by a quack doctor to relieve the pain from his worsening spinal defect. He married Billie Jean Jones of Bossier, Louisiana, "to spite Audrey."

Weather conditions prevented him from making a New Year's Eve show in Charleston, West Virginia. So Hank hired Charles Carr, a teenage cab driver, to drive him from Knoxville, Tennessee, where he had stopped for the night, to Canton, Ohio, for a New Year's Day booking there. After an injection for pain from a Knoxville physician, Hank got into the back of his Cadillac with a bottle of whiskey and a bottle of the pills his quack doctor had given him. Carr drove an hour and was stopped by a State Trooper who thought Hank looked dead, but was assured by Carr that he was sleeping as a result of his medication. When Carr stopped for gas five hours later in Oak Hill, West Virginia, he discovered that Hank was cold and limp. Hank Williams was pronounced dead, at age twenty-nine, at Oak Hill Hospital.

Hillbilly Humanism

The canon of Hank's songs covers a broad range of human experience. Hank wrote and sang all types of country songs—honky-tonk, cheatin' songs, blues, hillbilly laments, novelty songs, cajun-inspired numbers, train songs, and gospel songs. The vast majority of Hank's songs treat the subject of romantic love—especially love gone wrong.[4]

Chet Flippo, one of Hank's biographers, identifies a deep inner conflict in Hank's life and mind:

> He never really got it straightened out in his mind whether he was writing for Saturday night...or whether he was writing for Sunday morning.... He

---

[4] See the list in Curtis Ellison, *Country Music Culture: From Hard Times to Heaven* (Jackson: University Press of Mississippi, 1995) 274–78

kept writing both kinds of songs and could never get it entirely straight in his own mind just where he belonged. He wanted to have Saturday night every night, drink it up and have a good time but then he'd start to feel guilty and want to go back to Sunday morning and the sunlight and the white church and innocence.[5]

The known details of Hank's early life do not go far enough in explaining this tension. But both poles of Hank's inner conflict are clearly evident in his work—his songs.

Perhaps a comparison of the themes expressed in Hank's gospel songs with those of his "secular" songs and with those of more traditional gospel songs will illumine the conflicting impulses of his psyche. By my count, Hank wrote nineteen gospel songs. In addition, many if not most of Hank's "Luke the Drifter" songs fall into what might be called, to adapt Teresa Goddu's description, the "hillbilly gothic" tradition,[6] and a number of these have strong gospel overtones. Many of Hank's "secular" songs employ religious language.

Steve Goodson, in an essay titled "Hillbilly Humanist: Hank Williams and the Southern White Working Class," argues that Hank functioned, like black blues singers, as a "secular preacher," giving his audience "a strong sense of shared hardship and suffering, providing them at once with reassurance, emotional catharsis, and a measure of fellow-

---

[5] Flippo, *Your Cheatin' Heart*, 49.

[6] Teresa Goddu, "Bloody Daggers and Lonesome Graveyards: The Gothic and Country Music," *South Atlantic Quarterly* 94 (Winter 1995): 57–80.

ship."[7] Goodson contrasts the message of Hank's gospel songs with that of his secular songs. In the gospel songs, according to Goodson, Hank offers the hope of heavenly rewards as a palliative for the relentless suffering people experience in this life. Hank's gospel songs are "grim," but optimistic—life is "bleak," but one can choose a better way through faith in Jesus. In the secular songs, however, Hank is "unyieldingly" pessimistic. Persons are doomed to suffer, primarily through failed romantic relationships, and they are powerless to change their state of affairs. Moreover, according to Goodson, Hank presents contrasting views of God's providence. In the gospel songs, God is ever-present, listening for the prayers of sinners who want to come home. But in the secular songs, God is absent: "God does not even seem to exist—in day to day life outside the church."[8]

Goodson concludes that, collectively, Hank's songs express a philosophy that might be called "Hillbilly Humanism." This philosophy begins with a "Christian-based" affirmation of the dignity of persons, not unlike liberation theologies' preferential option for the marginalized, expressed most explicitly in songs like "Wealth Won't Save Your Soul" and "Mansion on the Hill."[9] A person's worth derives solely from his or her humanness and is not augmented by improvements in socio-economic status. In fact, Hank and his audience seem implicitly to understand

---

[7] Steve Goodson, "Hillbilly Humanist: Hank Williams and the Southern White Working Class," *Alabama Review* 46 (April 1993) 114.

[8] Ibid., 123.

[9] The lyrics to Hank's songs are found, arranged alphabetically by song title, in Don Cusic, ed., *Hank Williams: The Complete Lyrics* (New York: St. Martins, 1993).

that wealth and power tend to decrease the humanness of those who misuse them. In this light, the complaints in Hank's love-gone-wrong songs can be seen as protests against violations of the protagonist's human dignity. Hank's convictions about human dignity are seen also in his personal resentment of those who treated him differently after he became famous than they had when he was penniless. He knew he was still the same person: his money and success made him no better than anyone else, and certainly no better than he had been when he was poor.

But standing in constant tension with Hank's affirmation of human dignity is the lived awareness of social inequality. Hank's people—the Southern, white working poor—could not help but be aware of the differences between people in society, no matter how strong their conviction that all people are equal before God. So Hank's hillbilly humanist philosophy contains a deep, Orwellian, irony: all people are created equal, but some are more equal than others. Hank's music resonates with his poor white listeners because of its realistic assessment of the bleakness of redneck life. Hank's realism is seen in his strong awareness of the need for escape from daily suffering. Goodson sees the carnivalesque themes of Hank's honky-tonk songs as representing a temporary escape,[10] while the heaven of Hank's gospel songs represents a permanent one.

This sense of irony at the heart of Hank's musical outlook is a hallmark of all great country music. Goodson points out that one implication of this tension in Hank's life

---

[10] See also Stephen A. Smith and Jimmie N. Rogers, "Saturday Night in Country Music: The Gospel According to Juke," *Southern Cultures* 1 (1995): 229–44.

and work is a questioning of the puritanism/hedonism dichotomy so often applied to redneck culture. Both impulses existed simultaneously in Hank and, Goodson incurs, in the members of Hank's audience. Moreover, the contradictory impulses fermenting in the redneck community are testimony not to rural Southerners' lack of self-discipline and impulse-control, as popular stereotypes might suggest, but to the effects of their marginalization. Sample points out that such contradictory impulses continue to be characteristic of working-class life and that they reflect the difficulty of coming to terms with dehumanizing economic forces over which one has no control.[11]

But Goodson overstates the distinctions between Hank's secular and gospel songs. As I mentioned above, a number of Hank's songs—particularly the "Luke the Drifter" pieces—fall precisely into neither category. For example, "The Funeral," set in an African-American church, reinforces, though somewhat grotesquely, the gospel song tradition's dualism and other-worldliness. Another Luke the Drifter recitation, "Be Careful of Stones that You Throw," makes no explicit mention of religion, but obviously alludes to the New Testament letter of James and the gospel of John in presenting its moralistic message. Moreover, Hank's gospel songs are not as hopeful as Goodson implies, and his secular songs are not free of religious imagery. "Ramblin' Man," for example, describes its protagonist's ramblin' nature as foreordained by God, while "Lost Highway" and "You Win Again" explain their protagonists' fated difficulties in terms of sin and it wages. This same fatalism, expressed in

---

[11] Tex Sample, *White Soul: Country Music, the Church, and Working Americans* (Nashville: Abingdon Press, 1996) 93.

classics like "Cold, Cold Heart" and "I'll Never Get Out of this World Alive," along with the inevitable retributive justice evoked in "Your Cheatin' Heart," can be seen as having a transcendent locus. A doctrine of redneck karma—inexorable fate—is at work in Hank's songs of lost love and wasted life.

Hank's gospel songs, on the other hand, actually offer very little hope of redemption or release from life's troubles. In "House of Gold," for example, Hank sings: "I'd rather be in a cold dark grave/ and know that my poor soul is saved/ Than to live in this world in a house of gold/ and deny my God and doom my soul." What is notable about this eerie refrain is the absence of any mention of heaven. As discussed in the previous chapter, Christians singing in the gospel song tradition look forward to passing the next life in a city bright and fair, not a grave cold and dark. A similar tone of gloom is evoked in "We're Getting Closer to the Grave Every Day." Even Hank's most famous gospel song, "I Saw the Light," lacks movement toward a better future: the conversion experience is repeated thrice, as if it didn't take the first two times.

Leppert and Lipsitz point out that Hank's gospel songs embody a this-worldliness similar to black gospel music, contrary and even subversive to the otherworldly passivity of white gospel music.[12] The heart of Hank's gospel message is not the hope of heavenly bliss, but the loneliness and pain of life. Even Jesus is portrayed as a lonesome sufferer with whom other lonesome sufferers should, but apparently don't,

---

[12] Richard Leppert and George Lipsitz, "Age, the Body, and Experience in the Music of Hank Williams," in *All that Glitters: Country Music in America*, edited by George H. Lewis (Bowling Green OH: Bowling Green State University Popular Press, 1993) 25.

find communion. In "Calling You," "Jesus Died for Me," "Jesus is Calling," and "How Can You Refuse Him Now?" a graphically desperate Jesus implores desperate sinners to come to him. The tone of despair in these songs seems to assume that the sinners will not respond. The "Long-Gone Lonesome Blues," in fact, could be sung as easily about Jesus as about a woman. This utter loneliness at the core of human existence is not mitigated by Hank's dim hope for heavenly recompense.

Death by Baptism

Reading Hank's gospel songs in the context of his life highlights the tragedy of his quest for faith. The story is well known of his confession to Minnie Pearl that he hadn't seen any light after all. He sang that he'd rather be in a cold, dark grave than live in a house of gold, but a house of gold is where he lived, presumably believing he had denied his God and doomed his soul. His declaration in one of his more hopeful gospel songs—"When I get to glory, I'm gonna sing, sing, sing!"—merely promises an extension of what Hank knew this side of glory. Flippo concludes that Hank "was a weak man who found temporary salvation from his pain only when he was inside a song, a bottle, or a woman."[13] Perhaps his most hopeful longing was to be eternally inside a song.

The world of Hank Williams is bleak. Governed by an inexorable fate that is most concretely evident in the hopelessness of love relationships, life's only remedy is the death by immersion promised in the third verse of "Long-Gone Lonesome Blues," where the protagonist pledges to

---

[13] Flippo, *Your Cheatin' Heart*, 239.

sink "three times" into an ice-cold river but emerge only twice. This baptismal suicide, which so chillingly parallels the ending to Flannery O'Connor's short story, "The River," is Hank's strongest hope. Yet, despite life's bleakness, it is to be lived with humor. Hank's sense of humor and irony—playfully expressed in novelty songs like "Kaw-liga" and "Jambalaya," poignantly so in the sardonic wit of "Mind Your Own Business," "Why Don't You Love Me Like You Used to Do," "You're Gonna Change (Or I'm Gonna Leave)," "My Bucket's Got A Hole In It," and "Ill Never Get Out of this World Alive"—parallels that found in the blues. The stance toward life advocated in Hank Williams's songs straddles the gloomy recognition that we are indeed getting closer to the grave every day and the ironic awareness that none of us will ever get out of this world alive.

The directness of Hank's suicidal impulse reveals one example of the inanity of Tichi's approach to country music. Tichi, basing her analysis solely on "I'm So Lonesome I Could Cry," suggests that Hank upheld a secret pact with his listeners to entertain suicidal thoughts but not speak of suicide directly.[14] While it is true that Hank's pessimism stands in stark contrast to the optimism usually ascribed to American popular culture of the 1950s,[15] songs like "Long-Gone Lonesome Blues" make clear that Hank did not shrink from directly addressing socially questionable themes such as suicide. Ironically, Tichi's failure to listen closely enough to "Long Gone Lonesome Blues" also precludes an opportunity

---

[14] Cecilia Tichi, *High Lonesome: The American Culture of Country Music* (Chapel Hill: University of North Carolina Press, 1994) 101.

[15] See Kent Blaser, "'Pictures from Life's Other Side': Hank Williams, Country Music, and Popular Culture in America," *South Atlantic Quarterly* 84 (1985): 12–26.

to draw the kind of parallel she likes to draw between country music and more highbrow literature—a noteworthy one in this case, given the parallels between Hank's background and the world of Flannery O'Connor's fiction.

Tichi's offhand remark that "Hank Williams was baptized Hiram"[16] further demonstrates the inadequacy and insensitivity of her interpretation. She makes this remark to cite an example of country singers using Western-sounding monikers rather than their real names (does "Hank" really sound more "Western" than "Hiram"?). It apparently does not occur to her that, in the Baptist and Pentecostal environs of Hank's early life, infants are not dressed in white gowns and ceremonially sprinkled with water the way they would be in Tichi's high church New England world. In the low-church traditions of Hank's environment, baptism comes as a result of an individual's choice to leave the lost highway for the straight and narrow way. To my knowledge, Hank was never baptized at all; consequently, the question of his status before God haunted him throughout his life and worked its way into his music. The hopelessness of life in this world increases the likelihood that the life to come will be made the focus of the working-class pursuit of gratification. Thus the assumption that one is individually responsible for choosing one's eternal destiny is a hallmark of Southern rural culture that distinguishes it from more elite cultural circles where religious choices are more marginal in significance.

Hank's core theological affirmations of the dignity of persons and the hopelessness of life embody the contradictions experienced by poor working class and rural Southerners. Like a blues singer, Hank effectively rejects the

---

[16] Tichi, *High Lonesome*, 115

shallow and disembodied hope of the gospel of heaven and seeks instead a way to affirm life in its embodied earthiness. But Hank's break with religion is not as complete as that of the blues. Cone concludes that the blues side-step religion: "It is not that the blues reject God; rather they ignore God by embracing the joys and sorrows of life, such as those of a man's relationship with his woman, a woman with her man."[17] Hank does embrace the joys and sorrows of life, but he neither rejects nor ignores God. Instead, he continually pleads with God, as with an unfaithful lover, for mercy and relief from suffering. So Hank shares the blues' "stubborn refusal to go beyond the existential problem and substitute otherworldly answers,"[18] because Hank's version of heaven is neither a substitute nor a compensation for earthly suffering. But Hank's redneck version of the blues is not entirely this-wordly either. Death functions in Hank's songs the final relief from suffering and as the anticipated limit that assures us that our suffering is not infinite and thus helps to make suffering bearable.

Pilgrims on the Lost Highway: Hank's Legacy

Ellison notes that, in living out the archetypal image of "tragic troubador" and the theme of "domestic turmoil," Hank stands not alone, but in the distinct lines of country music tradition.[19] Prior to Hank, Jimmie Rodgers had been a lonesome drifter on the lost highway who, like Hank, would

---

[17] James Cone, *The Spirituals and the Blues* (Maryknoll NY: Orbis, 1992) 99.
[18] Ibid.
[19] Curtis Ellison, *Country Music Culture: From Hard Times to Heaven* (Jackson: University Press of Mississippi, 1995).

die an untimely death. A. P. Carter, "head" of the first family of country music, had prefigured Hank's domestic troubles. But Hank embodied these motifs more profoundly. Because of his popularity and the mythic dimensions his persona took on after his death, the tortured, lonesome, restless drifter has been fixed as a paragon of authentic country music.

In the ensuing years, paying homage to Hank by covering his songs, alluding to him or his songs either lyrically or stylistically, and singing about him have become standard ways that artists demonstrate their belonging within the country music community. Alan Jackson, Marty Stuart, and David Allen Coe have all had hits with songs about encounters with Hank's ghost. Such songs parallel early Christian accounts of Christ's resurrection appearances in that they amount almost to claims of divine revelation and apostolic commissioning in country music tradition.[20]

Another way artists pay homage to Hank is by drinking or otherwise anesthetizing themselves to or beyond the brink of death. George Jones went this route, but managed to avoid going over the brink. Hank, Jr. sings of his legacy of getting "stoned" in "Family Tradition," ironically the song that established him as an artist in his own right rather than someone trying to fill his father's boots. Country music's core audience testifies that Hank Williams wrote all of our lives. Hank's work, which expresses the struggles through which Hank himself lived, is seen to embody the struggles of Hank's people—the rednecks.

---

[20] Christopher Metress analyzes the way the Hank Williams myth has grown through tribute songs by other artists in "Sing Me a Song About a Ramblin Man: Visions and Revisions of Hank Williams in Country Music," *South Atlantic Quarterly* 94 (Winter 1995): 7–27.

The Gospel According to Hank

The artist who soon emerged as the heir apparent to Hank's mantle as tragic troubadour, domestic warrior, and premier country singer is George Jones. If Tichi's comparison of country artists to literary figures has any merit, then, as I suggested above, Hank Williams could be compared to Flannery O'Connor. But to whom could we compare George Jones? Jones's personal life has shown a self-destructiveness similar to Hank's. And in Jones's best work as an artist, the fatalism and pessimism of Hank Williams are magnified to almost macabre dimensions.

Kurt Vonnegut suggests that stories can be graphed according to their protagonists' movements between good fortune and ill fortune. The plot of most popular stories, according to Vonnegut, involves some transition from ill fortune to good fortune. In a Franz Kafka story, however, the plot begins with the protagonist facing ill fortune, and then things get worse, plummeting to infinity on the ill-fortune scale.[21] If Vonnegut's characterization rings true, then George Jones is the Kafka of country music. Jones is widely regarded as the greatest country vocalist ever.[22] Waylon Jennings asserts that other artists believe Jones's voice is the quintessential country music voice: "If we could all sound like we wanted to, we'd all sound like George Jones."[23]

---

[21] Kurt Vonnegut, *Palm Sunday: An Autobiographical Collage* (New York: Delacorte, 1981) 312–14.

[22] Ellison, *Country Music Culture*, 138; Nick Tosches, "George Jones: The Grand Tour," in *The Country Reader: Twenty Years of the Journal of Country Music*, edited by Paul Kingsbury (Nashville: Vanderbily University Press, 1996) 142–43.

[23] Waylon Jennings, quoted in Tosches, "George Jones," 142. See also Waylon Jennings with Lenny Kaye, *Waylon: An Autobiography* (New York: Warner, 1996) 353–58.

Producer Billy Sherrill has described Jones's voice as "a great primal scream of sorrow."[24] Jones sings songs about people who face the misery Hank portrayed by burying themselves deeper into misery.

For instance, the song "Why Baby Why"—his first hit—which portrays a mood of pessimism and fatalism in romantic relationships similar to what one would expect of a Hank Williams song, stands out as one of the more positive and upbeat numbers on Jones's "Super Hits" collection. Preceded by "White Lightning," one of the album's two novelty songs, "Why Baby Why" is reminiscent in style and content of Hank's "Why Don't You Love Me Like You Used to Do." It is followed by five songs that cumulatively portray an almost unbearable downward spiral of misery. The first of these, "The Window Up Above" tells the story of a man who watches helplessly from an upstairs window as his unfaithful wife embarks on an illicit rendezvous. Then the really sad songs start. In "A Picture of Me (without You)," Jones slowly and plaintively asks listeners to picture a series of increasingly gloomy metaphors of the loneliness of one who has lost his lover, culminating with the shattering "If you've watched as the heart of a child breaks in two/ then you've seen a picture of me without you." Next is "The Grand Tour," which Bill Malone, the dean of country music historians, suggests may be the greatest honky-tonk tearjerker ever—a room by room description of "an empty house" mercilessly stripped of joy and hope by the permanent departure of the protagonist's wife.

Following "The Grand Tour" is the title song from Jones's "Bartenders Blues" album. This song, perhaps

---

[24] Quoted in Ellison, *Country Music Culture*, 141.

Jones's finest vocal performance, resonates with a mournful desperation on the verge of exploding. The protagonist confesses his need to be surrounded by "four walls," lest he lose his sanity. Finally, there's the song that was voted the number one country song of all time by *Country America*, the only song to be named CMA Song of the Year twice—"He Stopped Loving Her Today." It took Jones eighteen months to record the song during a period in which he reached his lowest point in his legendary personal struggles with the demons of self-destruction[25]. It tells the story of a man who continues steadfastly in unrequited love until the day the undertakers come to "carry him away" for burial.

Like Hank, Jones identifies romantic love as a crucible in which persons encounter powers that *can* make life worth living but are more likely to do the opposite and strip life of any possibility of joy or hope. But, while Hank's protagonists find relief from their misery at death, Jones allows the suffering to linger until burial—or beyond. The jilted lover on the embalming table is "soon" to lay his sorrow to rest; the desperate bartender entombed within the four walls of a smoke-filled honky-tonk may wallow in his misery forever. The theme of burial is evoked also in the funerary style and imagery of "A Good Year for the Roses," as well as in the lesser known "A Place Out in the Country," which tells the story of an urban worker whose lifelong dream of moving to the country is realized only when he is buried in a rural graveyard.

The longing to be buried that Jones expresses in his music parallels his campaign in his own life to bury his *self* beneath "a river of booze, a bushel of cocaine." His

---

[25]See Ellison, *Country Music Culture,* 140–43.

autobiography in titled, *I Lived to Tell It All*.[26] But, as Bob Allen, who wrote an earlier biography of Jones, points out, "You can't tell it if you don't remember it."[27] Jones is forced to rely on secondary sources in his own autobiography because so much of his experience is buried somewhere beneath and beyond his own memory. Fortunately, Jones's story has a happier ending than Hank's. Jones managed finally to emerge transformed from an encounter with the ultimate in the crucible of romantic love, and he has credited his fourth and present wife, Nancy Sepulveda, for empowering him to become and remain clean and sober. Yet a near-fatal 1999 automobile accident, in which alcohol was implicated, calls into question Jones's claims of sobriety. Interpreters of country music—particularly those who see country music as poetry for the common man—want to draw a connection between the demons that drive Jones to drink and the depth of expression in his singing. Yet the precise nature of the demons that have driven Jones to self-destruction remains a mystery, perhaps irrecoverably buried within or beneath his self or perhaps merely a strong genetic predisposition to addictive behavior.

The sinister self-destructiveness embodied in the darker side of the lives and music of both George Jones and Hank Williams suggests a sinister seed within the core of country music. Perhaps such seemingly irrational yearnings are a logical corollary to being a member of a social group that is oppressed but not consciously aware of it. In the absence of a

---

[26] George Jones with Tom Carter, *I Lived To Tell It All* (New York: Villard, 1996).

[27] Bob Allen, review of *I Lived to Tell It All,* by George Jones with Tom Carter, *Journal of Country Music* 18/3 (1996): 41–43.

language with which to analyze the experience of suffering, the effects of illogical suffering are embodied and evoked in seemingly irrational impulses. Listeners should listen not merely to specific "sins"—such as drunkenness, sexual infidelity, or suicide—mentioned or advocated in the music, but also to the contradictory moral context that makes such acts seem to be a natural consequence of the protagonists' situations.

The best country music always embodies this tension between the way things ought to be (as in Hank's advocacy of the equal dignity of all persons) and the way things are (the dehumanizing forces that wrack working-class existence). Thus, most great country songs carry a strong sense of irony. This sense of irony is evident in the way many country song lines and titles seek to be humorous by relying on puns or twists of familiar expressions: "She Got the Gold Mine (I Got the Shaft)," "I'm the Only Hell My Mama Ever Raised," "The Power of Positive Drinking," "Friends in Low Places," "Cry on the Shoulder of the Road," "Pick Me Up on Your Way Down,"

The irony of country music is evident not only in the songs themselves, but also in the industry as a whole. To remain true to its traditions, country music must continue to make contact with its core audience by embodying the philosophy of hillbilly humanism. In other words, country must continue to be the music of a marginalized minority. But country music is also pulled in opposing directions. As consumer products of advanced capitalism, country recordings must continually broaden their appeal in order to increase their sales; country must appeal to music consumers in the cultural mainstream. So country music must be marginal and mainstream at the same time.

This tension too was at work in Hank's career. Hank undeniably voiced the feelings and concerns of his people. But he also appealed to the cultural mainstream. Not only was he wildly popular, but many of his songs were covered by pop artists and became hits on the pop music charts. Flippo's account portrays Hank as deeply ambiguous regarding his dual appeal. While he took pride and pleasure in having his songs become pop hits, he worried about losing touch with the common folks and found that the social climbers with whom he and Audrey began to associate after their move to Nashville were not his "kind" of people.

The tension between country's two locations—in the mainstream and at the margins of popular culture—is as old as the earliest recordings in the genre(s) that have become known as country music. The first commercial recordings of "Old Familiar" tunes resulted in a 1920s competition over market share between Georgia millhand Fiddlin' John Carson and New York tenor Vernon Dalhart—sometimes with both artists releasing recordings of the same tune. But despite the music industry's frequent efforts to court a more sophisticated audience, country music's hard-core fans have remained faithful, and hillbilly humanist themes have continued to be expressed.

Another artist who carries on Hank's hillbilly humanist legacy, and whose stature equals that of Jones, is Merle Haggard. Haggard was born near Bakersfield, California, to a family of recent migrants from Oklahoma. He grew up facing the kinds of difficulties that displaced, working-class families faced during the Great Depression, including the death of his father when Haggard was nine years old. Haggard had a troubled youth, developed a history of petty crimes, and was incarcerated at San Quentin at age twenty.

His experiences in prison taught him that crime doesn't pay, and he was paroled in 1960 determined to stay straight. His marriage had fallen apart while he was in prison, but he had also discovered music. He began writing songs inspired both by his prison experiences and by his experience of poverty. His first big hit came in 1963 with "Sing a Sad Song," while his first number one hit was "I'm a Lonesome Fugitive." Haggard's songs put a unique twist on traditional country music themes. For example, in one of his earliest songs—"The Bottle Let Me Down"—Haggard explores country music's conventional portrayal of drinking as a remedy for heartache. But "The Bottle Let Me Down" indicates more directly than most drinking songs that the remedy does not work. Haggard's "If We Make It Through December" portrays the agony of poverty so wrenchingly that it makes Loretta Lynn's "Coal Miner's Daughter" seem like wishful thinking.

In songs like "If We Make It through December," "Working Man Blues," and "Big City," Haggard asserts the dignity of the poor and working class, thus expressing the core of country music's hillbilly humanist. Another song that asserts working-class pride is "Okie From Muscogee," Haggard's most controversial hit. Haggard apparently recorded the song somewhat as a parody—"Muskogie is the only place I don't smoke it," he would later say, referring to marijuana[28]—but it was received as an anthem. "Okie" struck a chord among red-blooded Americans angered by the

---

[28] Quoted in Alex Halberstadt, "Merle Haggard," *Salon.com* (November 14, 2000) http://dir.salon.com/people/bc/2000/11/14/haggard/index.html?pn=1 (August 21, 2002).

behavior of anti-war protesters in the Viet Nam era. "Okie" was followed by another jingoistic single, "The Fighting Side of Me." Songs like "Okie" and "The Fighting Side of Me" are the kind of songs that produce antipathy toward country music among more sophisticated listeners (though Ronald Reagan, then governor of California, issued Haggard a full pardon for his earlier felony conviction after "Okie"). Haggard himself wanted "Irma Jackson," a song about interracial romance, to be the next single after Okie, but the record company would not agree. In "Are the Good Times Really Over," Haggard displays a more critical patriotism. But "Okie" and "Fighting Side" do assert the dignity of rednecks and their values just as much as Haggard's other songs.

The combination of jingoistic patriotism and radical social criticism in Haggard's work provides a perfect illustration of what Tex Sample calls working-class political traditionalism. The working-class, according Sample, is neither "conservative" not "liberal" as those terms are generally understood. The working class is "traditionalist," which means they prefer to be "left the hell alone" to pursue the good life in the context of their own communities and values. As an expression of this traditionalism, country music will embody a resentment of government and an affirmation of traditional family and social values consistent with political conservatism, but also a resentment of wealth and an affirmation of equality and a critique of unfair labor practices consistent with political liberalism.

Through the 1990s, hillbilly humanist themes have continued to be prominent on the country airwaves. Alan Jackson, for example, celebrates the simple pleasures of working-class life in songs like "Chattahoochie," "Livin' on

Love," "Home," and "Little Bitty." Randy Travis sings of the nobility of the common folk in "Better Class of Losers" and in his cover of the Roger Miller classic, "King of the Road," as does John Anderson in "Country 'til I Die." Other songs address working-class frustrations with bitter irony as in Mark Chesnutt's "Somebody Paints the Wall" and Travis Tritt's "Lord Have Mercy on the Workin' Man"; with mild humor as in Garth Brooks's "Friends in Low Places" and "American Honky-Tonk Bar Association" and Joe Diffie's "If the Devil Danced in Empty Pockets"; or with outright satire as in Sammy Kershaw's "Queen of My Double Wide," Tracy Byrd's "Lifestyles of the Not So Rich and Famous," and George Jones's "High-Tech Redneck."

The authenticity of some of these more recent anthems of Foxworthy-esque redneck pride has been widely questioned, however. Market research shows that the country audience is, to borrow a line form Alan Jackson's satire of the music industry, "not as backwards as they used to be." Listening to redneck humor on the radio while driving one's SUV through the suburbs seems to be a leisure pursuit of a different order than crying in one's beer in a dingy smoke-filled bar while listening to Hank Williams express the joys and frustrations of his people. So we turn our attention now to an artist who stands at the head of the pack in country music's invasion of the upper middle class.

3

The Apocalypse According to Garth:

Riding toward the Postmodern Roundup

> Garth's whole life was in his eyes. He had a strange messianic gaze that was like a sonar radar that, once it latched onto you, did not let up until it worked its will.
> —Lawrence Leamer in *Three Chords and the Truth*

Garth sang the first song fairly well, but during the second, his voice fading out with each word, he turned around and told us to stop playing. He approached the microphone slowly, bowed his head, and sighed. "Folks," he began, too ashamed to lift his eyes from the stage floor, "I can't do this to country music." He was nearly in tears. "I'm sorry about this, but my voice is gone. I hope you all can forgive us."

I can't do this to country music. It was an odd thing to say, even for melodramatic Garth. It was as if Garth felt he were somehow jeopardizing the integrity of country music.

—Matt O' Meilia in *Garth brooks: The Road Out of Santa Fe*

I'm pretty sure Garth Brooks is the Anti-Hank.
—Kinky Friedman

During the 1990s, seismic shifts occurred in the world of country music. Country became the most popular of all radio formats. The audience of country radio was the best educated and most affluent of all radio audiences. Country had gone from being primarily the music of the down and out to being a music preferred by the up and in. No artist played a greater role in this shift in country music's popularity and social location than Garth Brooks. While Kinky Friedman may be a bit harsh in his judgment that Garth is the Anti-Hank, we must acknowledge that if country is the music of the rednecks, then many of Garth's fans are *nouveau rouge*. Like any innovator, Brooks both embodies and transcends the classic styles and themes of country music.

"I can't do this to country music," Garth had announced in a Tulsa, Oklahoma, honky-tonk, when his effort to sing through a bout of laryngitis failed. Garth was singing with Santa Fe, the Stillwater, Oklahoma, based country "dance-cover band" that he had formed and fronted during 1986 and 1987 just before his decisive move to Nashville and stardom. The story is recounted by Matt O' Meilia, Sant Fe's drummer who left the band just before Garth and the other members moved to Nashville, in his 1998 memoir *Garth Brooks: The Road Out of Santa Fe*.[1] Garth laments as if, by performing poorly, he himself could bring about the end of country music as we know it. Of course, by performing at all, Garth *has* done something big to country music. But what?

O' Meilia also recounts how, on an earlier occasion, Garth had predicted to another Santa Fe bandmate that he'd one day be "bigger than Hank Williams." While country's faithful might consider such ambition heretical or even blasphemous, Garth has indeed surpassed Hank and Elvis and everyone else except the Beatles in record sales. And, if not for the release of the Beatles 1998 *Anthology*, he would have passed them also and may yet by the time this book is in print. So, if Garth becomes bigger than the Beatles, who in turn were (as John Lennon once suggested, bringing on a hailstorm of controversy) bigger than Jesus Christ, then can the apocalypse be far behind?

At any rate, even if Brooks's impact on popular culture in general and country music in particular has been less than apocalyptic, his music certainly contains apocalyptic messages, and his self-image and the adulation of his fans border on being messianic. When one visits the *PlanetGarth* website, one is greeted by Ed McCurdy's 1950s folk anthem, "Last Night I Had The Strangest Dream," which describes a dream in which all the leaders of all the nations have "agreed to put an end to war"—a vision of the end consistent with the message of one of Garth's most clearly apocalyptic songs, "We Shall Be Free" (not to mention the original messianic

---

[1] Matt O'Meilia, *Garth Brooks: The Road Out of Santa Fe*. (Norman: University of Oklahoma Press, 1997).

prophet, Isaiah). Garth intends his music not only to entertain, but to change the world. His fan newsletter, after all, is titled *The Believer*. Fan postings on the *PlanetGarth* bulletin boards, like the website's regular columns, are most frequently testimonials about the difference Garth has made in the lives of individual fans. Garth has inspired in many fans something close to religious devotion, and fan discourse is peppered with quotes from his lyrics much the same way that popular evangelical Christian discourse is often peppered with snippets of scripture.

Chris Dickinson titles her *Journal of Country Music* reflection piece on Garth's 1997 Central Park concert, "Garth In the Park: Do You Recall What Was Revealed?"[2] Dickinson references, of course, the 1972 Don McLean hit "American Pie," with which Garth, joined by McLean, closed the Central Park show. The question raised by McLean, then Garth, then Dickinson—"Do you recall what was revealed?"—carries us also to the very meaning of the word "apocalypse."

Apocalypse? Now?

The word "apocalypse" means "uncovering" or "unveiling"—hence "revelation." In apocalyptic literature, something previously unknown is revealed. Narrowly construed, apocalyptic literature is a genre that developed within Judaism (and consequently, early Christianity) around the second century B.C.E. One characteristic of biblical apocalyptic literature is that its message is communicated

---

[2] Chris Dickinson, "Garth in the Park: Do You Recall What Was Revealed?" *Journal of Country Music* 20/1 (1999): 10-17.

through cryptic symbolism or even secret code. It is the cryptic nature of these texts that has left them open to unrestrained conjecture and wildly speculative interpretation throughout Christian history. Another characteristic of biblical apocalyptic literature is its chronological, cosmic, and ethical dualism. An absolute dichotomy is posited between this present age and the age to come, between the cosmic forces of evil and the cosmic forces of good, and between infidels and true believers. The apocalypse performs, as Charles Talbert notes, a "hortatory function." Readers/listeners are encouraged to become and/or remain faithful through the present difficulties in order that they might participate fully in the glorious age to come.[3]

While Jewish and early Christian apocalypses did not always reflect the perspective of the marginalized, they most often did. Thus, Elizabeth Schüssler Fiorenza notes that apocalyptic literature is largely about power relationships; the apocalypse reveals that the present system of domination by unjust powers is soon to be undone.[4] The increasing injustice of the present age is seen as a sign that the age must soon end and a new age of justice and peace be ushered in. Biblical apocalypse, then, is a literature of crisis; that is, it addresses a situation in which the faithful find themselves threatened and are urged to remain faithful with the promise that, despite appearances to the contrary, their God is still in control.

Theologians and literary critics have analyzed apocalyptic themes not only in the assortment of biblical,

---

[3] See Charles H. Talbert, *The Apocalypse: A Reading of the Revelation of John* (Louisville: Westminster John Knox Press, 1994).

[4] See Elizabeth Schüssler Fiorenza, *Revelation: Vision of a Just World* (Minneapolis: Fortress Press, 1991).

apocryphal, and pseudepigraphical texts that comprised the genre of Jewish/Christian apocalyptic between the second centuries B.C.E. and C.E., but also in a variety of literary and popular texts from other eras. For example, James Preston Byrd interprets the slave spirituals as "apocalyptic discourse" because, like biblical apocalyptic, the spirituals posit a world in which the oppressive realities of the present no longer hold sway. According to Byrd, "apocalyptic is a response to a challenge, a way for the faithful to live in the midst of threat." Like the Jewish community under persecution by Antiochus and the early Christians facing persecution by Domitian or Trajan, slave communities responded to their extreme oppression by creating texts that interpreted their present reality in terms of an understanding that God who sides with the oppressed is moving history toward a better day.[5] The spirituals, of course, lack either the absolute dualism or the mysterious symbolism of biblical apocalyptic. So the connection Byrd draws broadens the meaning of "apocalyptic."

In literary "apocalypse theory," the broadening of the meaning of apocalyptic obscures distinctions that biblical exegetes and church historians might want to uphold. Any text that relates *the end* can be interpreted as apocalyptic, so terms like "apocalyptic," "eschatological," "millennial" or "millenarian," and even "messianic" virtually collapse in meaning and become interchangeable. Even texts that predate the emergence of biblical apocalyptic have been included in the category of apocalyptic.

---

[5] James Preston Byrd, Jr., "The Slave Spiritual as Apocalyptic Discourse," *Perspectives in Religious Studies* 19 (Summer 1992), 199–201, 204–216.

A further broadening of the meaning of "apocalyptic" occurs as any narrative that places persons in situations of extremity is seen as somehow apocalyptic. It is, after all, in situations of extremity that the deepest meanings of life are "revealed" (even if revealed to be absent). As Mark Ledbetter notes, literary texts are interpreted as apocalyptic when "the restoration of self develops through a spiritual journey that involves violence and chaos that takes characters to the extreme of human endurance and, in turn, allows, even forces, self discovery." In such texts, "knowing about the world and self is born out of terror and crisis."[6]

As I trace apocalyptic themes in the music of Garth Brooks and other country artists, I will be informed by all of the above definitions of apocalyptic. Garth does employ some very strange metaphors from time to time, which might be seen to parallel the cryptic symbolism of biblical apocalyptic. And Garth conveys his own type of dualism. Garth sings with a sense of ending—an eschatological urgency. This eschatological urgency produces a strong hortatory element in Garth's songs. And Garth, like other country artists, portrays persons in situations of extremity—persons passing through chaos, terror, and crisis on a hopeful journey toward order.

---

[6] Mark Ledbetter, "An Apocalypse of Race and Gender: Body Violence and Forming Identity in Toni Morrison's *Beloved*," in *Picturing Cultural Values in Postmodern America*, edited by Doty (Tuscaloosa: University of Alabama Press, 1995) 159–60.

The Life and Times of Troyal Garth Brooks

Troyal Garth Brooks was born 7 February 1962, in Tulsa, Oklahoma.[7] He grew up in the Oklahoma City suburb, Yukon. Garth's mother, Colleen, had been a recording artist for a brief stint in the 1950s, singing regularly on Red Foley's *Ozark Jubilee* radio and television broadcasts. Garth's father worked for an oil company. Garth came of age, then, amidst the pop culture wastelands of the 1970s—the era of disco and leisure suits. His musical tastes were eclectic. He listened to rock bands like Kiss and Boston and folk-rock artists like James Taylor and Dan Fogleberg. He also listened to the country music his parents loved, which probably planted the seeds of Garth's conversion to country music when George Strait inaugurated the neo-traditionalist movement in 1981.

The hodgepodge of musical influences that shape Garth's work is one source of the constant criticism that he is not really "country." But one must recall that, during Garth's formative decade, country radio may not have been the best place to go if one wanted to hear fiddles and steel guitar. During the 1970s, country charts were dominated by the likes of Olivia Newton-John, John Denver, Kenny Rogers, and other "crossover" sounds, while pop charts featured country-rock groups like the Eagles alongside Southern-rock acts like

---

[7] Biographical information is culled from Matt O'Meilia, *Garth Brooks: The Road Out of Santa Fe*. (Norman: University of Oklahoma Press, 1997); Bruce Feiler, *Dreaming Out Loud: Garth Brooks, Wynonna Judd, Wade Hayes, and the Changing Face of Nashville* (New York: Avon Books, 1998); Lawrence Leamer, *Three Chords and the Truth: Behind the Scenes with Those Who Make and Shape Country Music* (New York: HarperPaperbacks, 1977), and the *PlanetGarth* website, www.planetgarth.com.

the Allman Brothers, the Doobie Brothers, the Charlie Daniels Band, the Marshall Tucker Band, Lynryd Skynryd, and Wet Willie. In addition, country "outlaws" like Waylon Jennings and Willie Nelson had pop hits with traditional country songs like "Good-Hearted Woman" and "Luckenback, Texas."

The range of Garth's musical influences is one factor that differentiates him from the earlier artists I've discussed. A suburban rather than rural upbringing is another. A third has to do with education. With her cosmetology certificate, Tammy Wynette stands out as a scholar among her generation of country artists; Hank Williams, George Jones, and Loretta Lynn failed to finish high school, while Dolly Parton was the first in her family to do so. Garth Brooks, on the other hand, earned a degree in marketing from Oklahoma State University. In essence, Brooks decided in college to become a country singer just as his classmates were deciding to become doctors, lawyers, teachers, and accountants. Whether the major subject area of his college education or some other factor deserves the credit, there can be no doubting his ability to market himself.

After graduation from college, Garth went to Nashville to pursue a recording career. Unprepared for what he encountered, he went back to the university town of Stillwater, formed a band, and began plotting his return to Nashville. His band, Santa Fe, played country and pop covers along with a few original songs in clubs catering to the college crowd as well as on the rural honky-tonk circuit. Garth and the band moved to Nashville in the spring of 1998, and, though Santa Fe disbanded, Garth soon landed a recording contract.

Garth's first album, *Garth Brooks*, was released in 1989. Its first single, "Much Too Young (To Feel This Damn Old)," which portrays the struggles of an aging rodeo cowboy, was a top ten country hit. The second single, "If Tomorrow Never Comes," is sung from the perspective of a man who watches his wife (or daughter?) sleeping and ponders whether he has expressed clearly enough how strongly he feels about her, given the possibility that his life could end at any moment. "If Tomorrow Never Comes" reached number one on the country charts and introduced audiences to what would become Garth's central theological theme: the exhortation to live with passionate engagement in whatever life brings. The third single, "Not Counting You," which did not fare as well on the charts, is an imitation of George Strait's Texas swing inflected "Unwound"—the song that inspired Garth's career choice. The fourth single, "The Dance," which reinforces the hortatory message of "If Tomorrow Never Comes," became Garth's first signature hit and propelled him to superstardom.

His second album, *No Fences*, released in 1990, built on the momentum of the first by producing four number one country singles: "Friends in Low Places," "Unanswered Prayers," "Two of a Kind, Workin' on a Full House," and "The Thunder Rolls." "Friends in Low Places," of course, became Garth's signature party song, and opened the country airwaves to songs by other artists employing Foxworthy-esque redneck humor. With the video for "The Thunder Rolls," Garth fomented a major controversy by adding a third verse in which the wife exacts revenge by shooting her husband and placing in the foreground graphic visual images of spousal abuse, thus shifting the meaning of the song from mere adultery (which, after all, is pretty standard country fare) to domestic violence. The two country video networks banned the video, which brought a bonanza of media attention and increased sales. Martina McBride credits Garth's "Thunder Rolls" video with creating the opportunity for her to explore domestic violence so vividly in her hit song and award-winning video, "Independence Day."

In 1991, as Garth was preparing to release his third album in the wake of the "Thunder Rolls" controversy, *Billboard* magazine, which compiles the sales charts that the entire recording industry uses as a standard, changed its method of counting sales. The old method had been to survey a group of "reporters"—distributors and record store employees—about what was selling. This method concealed several biases against country music. First, country music fans were less likely to shop in record stores than in mass merchandisers such as K-Mart and Wal-Mart. Second, country music was most often relegated to the less desirable back corners of a record store's retail space, so only consumers intentionally seeking a country recording would come across one. Third, record stores tended to employ younger rock and pop listeners who had little interest in keeping track of country sales.

The new method would take advantage of technology. A company called SoundScan would calculate sales based on a sampling of actual bar codes scanned at point of scale. Shortly after the advent of SoundScan, Garth Brooks's third album, *Ropin' the Wind*, made its debut at number one on both the country and pop charts. The same week, his two prior albums also appeared in the top ten. Garth himself was fully aware that recognition of his success could be attributed to the fact that an accurate accounting of country record sales had finally entered the music industry. When asked by Larry

King to what he owed his popularity, he replied, "God and SoundScan."[8]

The ensuing years have brought seven more albums of new music, many awards, well-publicized disputes and contract renegotiations with his record label, record-setting ticket sales on every concert tour, the Central Park concert (and its live broadcast by HBO), several primetime network television specials, a boxed-set re-release of his first six albums, a guest-host appearance on *Saturday Night Live*, and a two-CD live album. Garth Brooks is indeed a pop culture phenomenon. But, purists complain, is he really country?

As part of Nashville's class of 1989, Garth was carefully packaged as a "hat act" or "country hunk"—a young male performer who would look, dress, and sing like a cowboy. Feeling pressure to conform to his carefully constructed image, Garth was reluctant to include the very un-cowboy-like "The Dance" on his debut album, despite the fact that it was one of his personal favorites. But producer and musical guru Allen Reynolds fought for the song's inclusion, and Garth himself fought to have it released as the album's fourth single. The song's success made clear that Garth would define rather than follow major trends in the country music industry.

Many, perhaps most, of Garth's songs reflect either traditional country music styles or traditional working-class country music themes. "Friends in Low Places" speaks from the familiar premise of a common man whose lover has rejected him for a man of higher social status. "Two of a Kind, Workin' on a Full House" is an upbeat honky-tonk romp. And "American Honky-Tonk Bar Association" comes

---

[8] Reported in Feiler, *Dreaming Out Loud*, 186.

across as a higher octane Okie-from-Muskogee-spirited anthem. Garth also includes cowboy/rodeo themed songs on every album. Certainly, Garth puts a rock edge on his music, but it could be argued that his edgier sounds are closer to the spirit of the rough-edged roadhouse country that grew with the repeal of prohibition in the 1940s and 1950s than the sanitized "Nashville Sound" that dominated country music through the 1960s and 1970s.

"Purist" critics of Garth Brooks overlook several of the realities of country music that Peterson, Malone, and other analysts have made clear. First, country music has always been a commercial creation. Record companies were looking for a product to sell, and artists have always been willing to provide one, whether that meant dressing down as hillbilly rubes and acting out negative stereotypes for the sake of humor or dressing up as cowboys to portray a more heroic American ideal. Image and marketing have always been central to country music. Second, as noted in earlier chapters, country music has always been influenced by other musical styles. Third, country music has often had ambitions to reach beyond its working-class core audience. Even Hank Williams was pleased to have his songs recorded by pop artists.

Bruce Feiler suggests that country music is best understood as an exercise in the preservation of values.[9] Commercial country music grew during America's transition from a rural agrarian nation to an urban industrial one, and earlier country music reflects not simply a nostalgia for simpler times, but an effort to keep alive traditions and ways of understanding the world that were endangered by the changing social realities. Country music's Southern

---

[9] See Feiler, *Dreaming Out Loud*, 239–52.

regionalism had to do with the fact that it was primarily the distinctive ways of life of the rural South that were threatened by urban migration. Now America is undergoing another transition, from an industrial economy to a diverse, global, information and service economy, so country music is also in transition, seeking once again to preserve certain values in the face of changing times. Country music is no longer about region at all, but about trying to find a way to affirm values in the face of increasing social fragmentation and individualism. A closer analysis of themes in the music of Garth Brooks and other contemporary artists will clarify what those values are.

The Last Roundup:
Apocalyptic in Country Music

Garth, of course, is not the first artist to incorporate apocalyptic themes into country music. A number of country artists have recorded the kind of eschatological gospel songs I discussed in chapter 1. Early hillbilly acts like the Carter family moved freely back and forth across the boundary between sacred and secular and included eschatological gospel hymns in their repertoires. The boundary between sacred and secular, in fact, has never been boldly drawn in country music. The classic cowboy song, "The Last Roundup," is traditional Christian eschatology in cowboy boots, while Ferlin Husky's "The Great Speckled Bird" elaborates an obscure biblical apocalyptic image. In the 1970s, Willie Nelson's *The Troublemaker* album included apocalyptic numbers among its rough-edged honk-tonk renditions of gospel standards, while the Nitty Gritty Dirt Band had everyone wondering "Will the Circle Be Unbroken?" The Oak Ridge Boys, who left the world of

Southern Gospel to achieve mainstream country success, speculated about the reception Jesus might have if he returned during the 1980s in "Would They Love Him Down in Shreveport Today?" The acclaimed *Trio* album by Dolly Parton, Emmylou Harris, and Linda Ronstadt included not only that most theodical of the gospel hymns, "Farther Along," but also the equally eschatological "Angel Band" and "When They Ring Those Golden Bells for You and Me." On 1999's *Trio II*, they include Neil Young's "After the Gold Rush," of which Parton says, "I always thought this song was about the Second Coming or the invasion of space aliens." Collin Raye offers a post-Garthian approach to Christian eschatology in "What if Jesus Came Back Like That?" And the Judds, beginning a fifteen month publicity buildup anticipating their New Year's Eve 1999 reunion concert in Phoenix, use rhetoric about "the millennium" almost as if they expect the *parousia* itself to occur at their show.

Eschatological/apocalyptic themes likewise pervade country songs that lack explicit religious messages. Also prominent in the repertoires of the Carter Family and other early hillbilly acts were murder ballads, in which the apocalypse—the individual encounter with death—is up close and personal, as it is in Hank Williams's and George Jones's many songs about death. Other ballads, such as those emerging from the Amarillo based "cosmic cowboy" movement, present apocalyptic narrative journeys through extremity. The characters in Guy Clark's "Desperadoes Waiting for a Train" are also desperately waiting for a revelation, while the heroes of Townes Van Zandt's "Poncho and Lefty" (popularized by Willie Nelson) are moving steadfastly toward their end.

Even in songs about "home," an oft-visited theme in country music, an apocalyptic note can be heard. Home songs are often assumed to be expressions of nostalgia—romantic idealizations of a simpler golden age located somewhere in the past. I contend,[10] however, that the longing expressed in these songs is more often for a new future than for a lost past. Consider, for example, the Western standard "Home on the Range," the mother of all home songs. The protagonist of "Home on the Range" asks not for a return to some past simplicity, but for a new home on the new frontier—a cabin in the American Elysian Fields. Similarly, Bobby Bare's "Detroit City," despite its repeated chorus of "I want to go home," should not be read as a nostalgic longing for a simpler life once had but now lost. After all, it was the economic hopelessness of the rural home-place that prompted the song's protagonist to join the hillbilly migration to the economically oppressive urban North in the first place. Bare's hillbilly captive in Detroit, like the protagonist in Merle Haggard's "Big City," longs for a new home that will transcend both rural destitution and urban oppression. In other words, the longing for home in country music is eschatological more than nostalgic.

One striking example of a country-western apocalypse is Willie Nelson's *Red Headed Stranger*, the album that converted me to country music. The album's instrumental background is as sparse as the landscape of a post-apocalyptic science fiction film. Willie's guitar, a harmonica, a bass, a piano, and occasional drums move in and out of earshot,

---

[10] David Fillingim, "A Flight from Liminality: 'Home' in Country and Gospel Music," *Studies in Popular Culture* 20/1 (October 1997): 75–82.

while Willie's plaintive vocals stand squarely in the foreground. The "Time of the Preacher" theme, split into three segments interspersed throughout side one, forms the skeleton of an unfolding drama of love, betrayal, death, grief, and redemption. Willie begins the opening refrain by announcing, "It was the time of the preacher," leaving no doubt that a religious/spiritual message is forthcoming. The "Time of the Preacher" will indeed prove to be both *chronos* and *kairos*, the biblical fullness of time, as this "story" about "the choice of woman and the love of a man" unfolds. The time of the apocalypse is now, the opening refrain concludes, for "now the preaching is over, and the lesson's begun."

The next song, an up-tempo cheatin' song titled "I Couldn't Believe It Was True," hints at two important themes. First, the woman's "choice" introduced in the opening theme, we are now led to believe, will be revealed to involve infidelity. Second, the listener is invited to share and then transcend the protagonist's expressed incredulity—not only his incredulity regarding this woman's unfaithfulness, but also our potential disbelief at the apocalyptic message once it is fully revealed. The singer "couldn't believe it was true," but he and we know that it is. The second installment of the "Time of the Preacher" theme follows, picking up a third theme from "I Couldn't Believe It Was True," the failure to forgive, which moves the drama closer to the full realization of the apocalyptic moment: "Now the lesson is over, and killing's begun."

The next cut is a medley of two song fragments. The first fragment, "Blue Rock Montana" describes the murder of the unfaithful woman and her lover and is actually the first verse to a song whose second verse appears separately five cuts later. The second song fragment is the chorus to "Red

Headed Stranger," a song that later appears in its entirety. This medley represents a prefiguring of the apocalyptic revelation, the first coming for which "Red Headed Stranger" will be the *parousia*. After the "Blue Rock Montana/Red Headed Stranger" medley comes the album's hit single, "Blue Eyes Crying in the Rain," which, in its context on the album, serves as a funeral hymn expressing a longing for an eschatological reunion between the jilted lover and his murdered love.

In the album's title song the apocalyptic moment is revealed. The red-headed stranger, with "eyes like the thunder," rides into a new town, absorbed in his own inner chaos, a chaos that must be externalized and shared if it is to be resolved. The stranger has the riderless "bay pony" of his dead lover in tow behind his own "raging black stallion"—so this apocalypse has two horses rather than four. He picks up a woman at the saloon, then shoots her as she gestures to take the reigns of the bay pony. The song points out that the stranger will "of course" not be punished, there being no law against shooting horse-thieves, causing the listener to feel a bit duped. Is this a sermon or a burlesque? Or is there a difference? The moral of the story is to be watchful—the red-headed stranger could ride into any town, any time. Watchfulness is also the moral of most of the apocalyptic parables and teachings of the New Testament.

Lest anyone miss the apocalyptic message, the final installment of the "Time of the Preacher" theme follows, proclaiming: "Just when you think it's all over, it's only begun." The apocalyptic moment is not end only, but also beginning. That this new beginning is religious or spiritual in nature is confirmed as the final segment of "Time of the Preacher Theme" segues into an instrumental of Charlotte

The Apocalypse According to Garth 87

Elliott's classic evangelical invitation hymn, "Just as I Am." The hymn is followed by "Denver," which is actually the second verse of "Blue Rock Montana." Whereas Blue Rock had been where the adulterous lovers "died with their smiles on their faces," "Denver," the mile-high city, becomes the heaven hoped for in "Blue Eyes Crying in the Rain"—a place where the reunited lovers "danced with their smiles on their faces." The apocalypse has been revealed and the millennium has begun. Side one ends with a slowly fading instrumental of "Over the Waves," a song evoking a music box that never winds down.

Side two begins with a rousing piano instrumental, "Down Yonder," a song one might expect to hear after intermission at a saloon show, to signal that intermission has ended and the show is about to continue. Yet our story seems complete already. How can the apocalypse have a second half? In traditional Christian apocalyptic, eschaton is followed by millennium. In other words, the apocalyptic unveiling is not merely an end, but also a beginning. "Down Yonder" is followed on side two by three songs that can be read as prayers expressing the longing for immortality or for rest from life's troubles.

First, "Can I Sleep in Your Arms" equates the longing for solace from the troubles of life with the longing for female companionship, consistent with country music's tradition of marking romantic love as the locus of the experience of the divine. Next, "Remember Me (When the Candle Lights Are Gleaming)" asserts the desire to transcend the limits of mortality by living on in a lover's memory after a relationship (or perhaps life itself) ends. Finally, "Hands On the Wheel" is a song expressing quiet satisfaction in finding "something that's real"—a love that will last. Love is depicted as the prize at the end of a long spiritual journey toward self-realization: "I found myself in you." The album closes with another instrumental, "Bandera," which, like the number that ends side one, evokes a music box, or carousel perhaps, turning in unending bliss.

If Tomorrow Never Comes, Will I Still Have Friends in Low Places?

Garth Brooks's first single, "Much Too Young (To Feel This Damn Old)," introduces his apocalyptic message. This song's protagonist is an aging rodeo cowboy overwhelmed by a sense of the approaching end of his career. Though this song is too early to reflect Garth's own later obsession with the end of his singing career, I cannot help thinking of Michael Dunne's observation that many "cowboy" songs are in reality "self-referential" statements about the life of a traveling singer.[11] Brooks's second single (and first number one), "If Tomorrow Never Comes," intensifies this apocalyptic sense of ending and adds a hortatory plea. In this song, a man watches his wife (or daughter?) sleeping and is bothered by the thought that she might not really know how strongly he feels about her. The end could come anytime—could come even tonight—therefore, one must be sure to share one's feelings with loved ones before it's too late.

---

[11] Michael Dunne, *Metapop: Self-Referentiality in Contemporary American Popular Culture* (Jackson: University Press of Mississippi, 1992) 124–44.

In his next number one single, "The Dance," which Curtis Ellison correctly identifies as Brooks's core theological statement,[12] the protagonist reflects on the memory of a love that didn't last, recalls the pain, and concludes that it was worth it after all. In this song, Garth inverts the message of Hank Williams and George Jones by celebrating rather than cursing the fate that dooms romantic relationships. The hortatory message here is that passionate engagement in relationships—even those likely to bring hurt—is the only option worthy of consideration. To Garth, the dispassionate life is not worth living. In the explicitly theological "Unanswered Prayers," Garth again celebrates the fate of a failed romantic relationship, assigning a cosmic wisdom to the way things have worked out.

In the video version of "The Dance," the song's message is expanded to advocate passionate involvement not merely in romantic relationships, but in whatever life brings. The video features a parade of images of heroes and luminaries such as Martin Luther King, Jr., John Wayne, Keith Whitley, and the Space Shuttle *Challenger* crew. What all these people have in common is that they lived to the fullest—they followed their dreams, Garth might say. Personally, I find troubling the implication that drinking oneself to death is as laudatory as leading the civil rights movement. But what this song and its video introduce us to is Garth's own brand of apocalyptic dualism.

Classical apocalyptic literature is dualistic in that it tends to divide reality into separate binary spheres—good vs. evil, light vs. darkness, life vs. death, etc. The dualism of biblical

---

[12] Curtis Ellison, *Country Music Culture: From Hard Times to Heaven* (Jackson: University Press of Mississippi, 1995) 262–63.

apocalyptic, for example, is cosmic in scope and has ethical and chronological dimensions. Chronologically, an absolute dichotomy is established between this present evil age, which will soon pass away, and the future age of triumph to be ushered in with the impending apocalyptic cataclysm. Ethically, persons and forces are aligned with either the powers of good or the powers of evil—there is no gray area or middle ground.

Garth's dualism is not so stark. No dichotomy is constructed between the kind of polar opposites named in traditional dualisms. In fact, Garth's music holds such binary pairs together like the yin and yang of Taoist cosmology. Garth recognizes and makes completely clear what I discussed in Chapter One—that country music somehow melds the spiritual and the sexual. "Sometimes it's very, very filthy in what it talks about," Garth says of his music. "Sometimes it's as pure as, you know, a newborn baby in what it talks about."[13] This intermingling of sex and spirit also involves the confluence of eros and thanatos— of sex and death. Garth surmises: "That's me. My albums talk about God. My albums talk about sex. My albums talk about death."[14] God, sex, and death—spirituality is coupled with sexuality, passionate engagement in the present moment with intense awareness of an impending end.

Garth's core dualism is ethical, but is not the traditional ethical dualism of good vs. evil. Rather, Garth's dualism has to do with the stance one adopts toward life. It is a dualism between two styles of living—those who join "The Dance" vs. those who remain wallflowers; those who are passionately

---

[13] Quoted in Leamer, *Three Chords and the Truth*, p. 35
[14] Quoted in Feiler, *Dreaming Out Loud*, p. 194.

engaged in life vs. those who aren't. This dualism is repeated in Garth's songs. In "The River," those who "choose to chance the rapids" are contrasted with those who remain on shore. In "Standing Outside the Fire," those who take chances and risk love are contrasted with those who play it safe and are content to be independent. In "The Change," the one soul who ventures to make a positive difference in the world is contrasted with the "thousand more" who rest in their complacency believing that trying to make a difference would be useless. In "How You Ever Gonna Know," those who are willing to risk getting hurt or to appear foolish in pursuit of their dreams are contrasted with "critics who put their own dreams on the shelf."

The bitter irony is that both groups are headed toward the same end. Those who risk, who dance, who jump into the fire are risking annihilation. Yet those who play it safe risk dying without ever having lived. Garth stands then as a latter day Qoheleth, reminding us that we all are moving steadily toward the end. For Garth, in fact, the end is what gives life meaning, or at least motivation. The knowledge that life is short is sufficient reason for making the most of it. Tomorrow may never come, so don't waste today.

Brooks's core message of passionate engagement in life—in relationships especially—is evident throughout his work. Often, Garth emphasizes the intensity of passion itself as an irresistible force, as in "That Summer," "Ain't Goin' Down 'til the Sun Comes Up," and "The Red Strokes." Sometimes passion takes on an apocalyptic urgency. In "Papa Loved Mama," for example, Garth depicts the annihilation that lurks as a possibility when passions flare. Similarly, "Ireland" pays tribute to the heroism of soldiers willing to give their all in a battle they have no hope of winning. The sense of the urgency of expressing one's feelings, first introduced in "If Tomorrow Never Comes," is negatively recast in the cryptic "Beaches of Cheyenne," which offers a postmodern cowboy update of the hillbilly classic "Wreck of the Old 97" by warning listeners: be careful what you say to loved ones because you never know what words might be the last ones you speak to them.

A second key theme in Garth's music is community. If Feiler is right that 1990s country music is struggling with changes in the country's values, then Garth's plea is for unity and community in the face of an ever intensifying fragmentation of communal bonds. This yearning for community is expressed most directly in "We Shall Be Free," a Black-gospel-inflected song Garth co-wrote after watching smoke rise from the fires of the riots following the Rodney King verdict as his tour bus left Los Angeles. The message of community is also evident in Garth's more humorous songs; one finds solace in life by visiting with "Friends in Low Places" or consulting with the local chapter of the "American Honky Tonk Bar Association." In "Belleau Wood," a musical setting of the old preacher story about German and American soldiers together singing "Silent Night/ *Stille Nacht*" in the darkness one Christmas night during World War II, Garth contrasts the horror of war with the hope of peace and unity.

The importance of community is also seen in Garth's transformation of the cowboy image. Traditionally, the cowboy is a symbol of rugged individualism. The cowboy's heroism lies in his independence. But, in Garth's songs, the lone cowboy is a pitiable soul, incomplete and out of control. In "Cowboys and Angels," a retelling of the Genesis creation story, God creates woman because the lone cowboy could "never make it on his own." In "Rodeo," "Beaches of

Cheyenne," " Much Too Young (To Feel This Damn Old)," and other of Garth's cowboy songs, the cowboy is held up as a tragic figure—driven by impulses he cannot control and utterly alone and desolate.

The video of "The Dance" also suggests the importance of community. What the heroes whose images dance in the song's foreground have in common is not only their engagement in life, but also the fact that they all shared their lives and gifts with others. This theme of using one's life to make a positive difference in the world is carried forward in "The Change" (like "The Dance," composed by songwriter Tony Arata), which Garth offered as an anthem of sorts for the Oklahoma City bombing survivors. Garth has expressed a belief that music should not only entertain; it should make the world a better place.

Garth's community building efforts have not been above reproach. His schemes have at times appeared grandiose, as when he urged his management team to arrange for him to meet with President Clinton to develop a plan for achieving world peace, in the apparent belief that his music could succeed where diplomacy has failed. While he gained some praise from progressive circles for daring to challenge country music culture's homophobia in the lyrics to "We Shall Be Free," his openness overstepped appropriate boundaries when he thoughtlessly outed his lesbian sister on primetime television without her prior knowledge or consent. While supporters see his "Thunder Rolls" video and its accompanying charitable efforts as a positive contribution to raising awareness of and offering practical assistance for domestic violence, cynical critics see a mere marketing ploy.

Both of Garth's major themes—his advocacy of passionate engagement in life and his sense of the importance of community—are evident in his concert performances. The intense devotion of Garth's fans is bolstered by the intensity of his performances. Fans perceive that Garth gives his all for them every night. Garth himself sees the key to his success as a live performer in an intense connection that somehow unifies him and the audience. Garth's concerts have come to resemble religious services, ceremonies of communion on a grand scale. At times, Garth stands alone on stage playing his guitar and listening to the audience sing the lyrics—a choir of ten thousand voices joining to confess, "Sometimes I thank God for unanswered prayers." Most preachers would be proud to achieve this level of rapture among their congregants. The mystical union between performer and audience becomes the moment of truth.

The criticism of Garth, the questioning of his sincerity, reflects the conundrum of postmodern country music. Country music has always been commercial, but has for most of its history managed to retain some connection to rural, working-class simplicity as a mark of its authenticity—an unwritten "sincerity contract" exists between fan and artist.[15] Country artists make great efforts to emphasize their humble roots and remain accessible to their fans. Garth's devotion to fans is legendary. At "Fan Fair," the annual Nashville festival at which country music fans wait in long lines to meet and receive autographs from their favorite stars, Garth has been known to stand in his booth for hours on end without so much as a bathroom break. But maintaining that simplicity and accessibility after one has earned billions of dollars is difficult. Early in Garth's career, he was widely perceived as a fresh voice who sometimes dared to color outside the lines

---

[15] Tichi, *High Lonesome*, 210–21.

drawn by the music industry's image and marketing consultants. Soon he began to revel in and exaggerate his own iconoclasm so that he himself became to many a symbol of the cynicism of the capitalist machine. The problem for Garth and his generation is the hegemony of advanced capitalism, which reduces even sincerity to a marketable commodity.

Perhaps one way to gain insight into Garth's place in the country music pantheon is to compare his songs with similarly themed songs by another artist. It happens that on several occasions, George Strait has released singles with themes virtually identical to the themes of Garth's singles. Strait is a rancher turned artist who is widely acknowledged as a pioneer of neo-traditionalist country music; his sincerity and authenticity are seldom questioned. What accounts for Strait's music being considered unquestionably authentic while Garth's is subject to doubt? Consider the differences when both singers released Cajun-inflected numbers. Since Hank Williams sang "Jambalaya," it seems that every noteworthy country artist has felt obligated to pay homage to Cajun music. Garth's foray into Cajun was a cover of Nitty Gritty Dirt Band's hit "Calling Baton Rouge," done with vocals at a near scream at an excruciating pace that leaves the impression that the vocalist and the instruments are racing to see who can finish the song first. Garth's "Calling Baton Rouge" ends up sounding sort of like a heavy metal band trying to make bluegrass music. In contrast, Strait's Cajun hit was "Adelida," an up-tempo number performed in a straightforward manner with appropriate accent on the fiddles and accordion.

A similar difference is seen when the two sing about rodeo. Garth's first rodeo song was "Much Too Young (To Feel This Damn Old)" from his first album—the stage of

Garth's career when he often imitated Strait—and is rather straightforward traditional country. Garth returns to the rodeo theme in at least one song on every album, but only "Rodeo" from *Ropin' the Wind* and "The Fever" and "Beaches of Cheyenne" from *Fresh Horses* were singles. "Rodeo" is a rollicking up-tempo number with a rather heavy rock beat. "The Fever" (the Aerosmith cover) was Garth's biggest failure as a single, while "Beaches of Cheyenne," as its title suggests, is a strange song that defies categorization. Strait's best rodeo song is "I Can Still Make Cheyenne," a poignant and perfect ballad of a relationship dissolving because of the traveling life of a rodeo cowboy. Here Strait's performance and the production are understated, and the song speaks for itself.

Strait again attains country music perfection on "I Know She Still Loves Me (But I Don't Think She Likes Me Anymore)," a mid-life lament. Strait's understated performance is again perfectly transparent, as he avoids the temptation to elongate notes on the final chorus. The production is also commendable, as instruments are added one at a time, evoking the way layers of baggage get added to a relationship over time, then stopped short as Strait delivers the last line *a capella*. Garth's treatments of male mid-life appear excessive by comparison. "Much Too Young (To Feel This Damn Old)," after all, was released when Garth himself was not yet thirty. Excess, in fact, is one of Garth's distinguishing characteristics. Strait, along with other acknowledged traditional artists like Randy Travis and Alan Jackson, tend to sing in a straightforward understated style that allows the lyrics to carry the song. Garth, by contrast, engages in heavy metal inspired vocal pyrotechnics that sometimes distract from a song's message.

The Apocalypse According to Garth

In his 1999 project, *Garth Brooks In...The Life of Chris Gaines*, Brooks further exploits the fact that his work straddles the boundaries between country and rock. Garth poses as Chris Gaines, a fictitious rock star who is to be the subject of an upcoming movie by Red Strokes Productions (owned by Brooks) titled *The Lamb*. *The Life of Chris Gaines* is a collection of songs in various pop and rock styles allegedly culled from Gaines's previous albums, descriptions of which are included in accompanying publicity materials. The album was universally panned by critics and did not sell well, prompting some to speculate that Garth had overextended his creative ability. But loyal fans—those whose cyberselves populate the *PlanetGarth* website—were undeterred and expressed the same love for their hero's newest efforts as for the previous works. Some posts go as far as to allege an evangelistic duty of purchasing multiple copies of the Chris Gaines album to give as holiday gifts, accomplishing the dual purpose of increasing sales and spreading the message. Fans who have not purchased the Chris Gaines album are accused of disloyalty, perhaps even apostasy.

In an interview, Brooks dismisses the controversy over his adoption of Chris Gaines persona, explaining that the album is a pre-soundtrack intended to stimulate interest in the upcoming film and that he was merely acting. He agrees that country music is "going through an identity crisis" with the infusion of too many pop sounds, but does not see himself as contributing to that crisis. "We need more artists that are undeniably country like The Dixie Chicks," Garth states. "When that happens we will get our identity back, respect will come with it and we can grow again."[16] So, while he acknowledges his eclectic musical tastes and roots, Brooks insists that he is part of the "we" of the country music community—those "artists that are undeniably country"—not part of the "they" who are threatening the identity of "our" music.

Given Garth's ambition to be "bigger than Hank Williams," it is worthwhile to note that Hank also recorded under the name of an altar-ego, Luke the Drifter. Moreover, like Hank's Luke the Drifter, Chris Gaines is a persona through which the artist can explore darker themes than in his standard works. In addition, in both cases, one justification for adopting the altar-ego is to prevent audience confusion. In Hank's case, the Luke the Drifter works needed a different artist name so that jukebox distributors who assumed that all Hank Williams records were appropriate for honky-tonk play would not mistakenly add the mournful, moralistic, and quasi-religious recitations to their jukeboxes. Brooks states that he could never release a rock album under his own name because "that's just not what I do" and explains that one reason for keeping any rock persona he might project separate from his identity as a country artist is to avoid confusing fans who like only country music.

Theologically, it is important to note the themes of death and redemption in the mock bio of Chris Gaines. Gaines's best friend and bandmate is said to have died after their first album. Then his father dies of cancer after the second album. Finally Gaines himself suffers a near-fatal automobile accident, after which he goes into seclusion and releases an album titled *Apostle*. Both Feiler and Leamer report that

---

[16] From an interview posted at the *PlanetGarth* website.

Brooks himself spent long periods preoccupied with his own death and even fantasized at times about dying during a performance, becoming the ultimate sacrifice for his fans. That the forthcoming Chris Gaines movie is titled *The Lamb* suggests a connection with Brooks's own messianic sacrificial impulses. The pseudonym itself suggests a confluence of the two major cultural influences behind country music: Christianity and capitalism.

Time will determine whether Garth Brooks has brought innovations that will leave a permanent stamp on country music, or whether he is better understood as the leading artist in another of country music's cyclical variations between hardcore and soft shell sounds. Other recent artists have followed Garth's lead in a variety of ways. John Michael Montgomery repeats Garth's message of passionate engagement in life (and even borrows Garth's metaphor) in "Life's a Dance." A number of artists have expanded on the type of humor Garth displays in "Friends in Low Places," "Two of a Kind (Workin' On a Full House)," and "American Honky Tonk Bar Association." Redneck chic is caricatured in Joe Diffie's "Pick-Up Man" and "Prop Me Up Beside the Jukebox If I Die," Tracy Byrd's "Lifestyles of the Not So Rich and Famous," Sammy Kershaw's "Queen of My Double Wide," Confederate Railroad's cover of Jerry Jeff Walker's "I Like My Women a Little On the Trashy Side," Diamond Rio's "Bubba Hyde," Kenny Chesnee's "She Thinks My Tractor's Sexy," and a number of other songs. More and more country artists are putting a rock edge to their music. While Garth stands as the most visible leader in this regard, the influence of the Eagles, Linda Ronstadt, and the Southern Rock movement (imported into 1990s country music by Travis Tritt among others) must also be acknowledged.

Other artists continue to sing about traditional working-class country themes. Aaron Tippin brags about a "Working Man's Ph.D." Tracy Byrd proclaims, "I'm from the Country and I Like It That Way." But traditional working-class country is often crowded out of the country airwaves by the more rock-oriented sounds emanating from artists like Garth and the pop-oriented music of teenage artists like LeeAnne Rimes, Lila McCann, Bryan White, and others who represent the industry's efforts to attract the ever-coveted youth audience. If the pattern Peterson detects in country music history holds true, rock and pop sounds will diminish (as will country's share of the radio market), and traditional hardcore artists will regain dominance. Only time will tell what Garth Brooks's lasting influence will be.

Whatever his place in country music history may prove to be, Garth certainly delivers a theological message for changing times. Garth answers the individualism of the age with a call to community. More significantly, he answers the alienating effects of social fragmentation with a plea for involvement—for passionate engagement in the rhythms of life. Garth calls listeners to the altars of intimate relationships and passionate living. Tomorrow may never come. So dance today. Swim the river. Jump into the fire. Change the world. Be free. And remember that you have friends in low places.

4

Stand by Your Man and Your Daughters Shall Prophesy:

The Emergence of Honky-Tonk Feminisim

> I will pour out my Spirit on all flesh, and your sons and your daughters shall prophesy.
> —the prophet Joel as quoted by the apostle Peter in Acts 2:17

> I'm not a big fan of women's liberation, but maybe it'll help women stand up for the respect they're due.... Most of my songs were from the woman's point of view.
> —Loretta Lynn in *Coal Miner's Daughter*

The classic country hit "Stand By Your Man" has been much maligned as *the* anthem of feminine passivity, while its singer, Tammy Wynette has become an icon of female submissiveness. Wynette's advocacy on behalf of conservative political causes has further reified her own reputation as a champion of traditionalism and has added to the perception that country music as a whole is the mouthpiece of reactionary politics. But is country music—particularly the music of female artists like Wynette—really as anti-feminist as is generally assumed? After all, Wynette's other hits include "Cowboys Don't Shoot Straight Like They Used To" and "I Don't Wanna Play House." Even "Stand By Your Man" portrays women as the stronger of the sexes: women must "stand by" because men, like the lower animals, are incapable of moral agency. "After all, he's just a man," Wynette sings.

In some ways, women's country music has traveled its own road, somewhat separate from the music made by men before, during, and after the emergence of commercial country music. Prior to country music's commercial development, men's and women's musical practices diverged in the hills and hollers where traditional music lived. Men's music was public music, the devil's music, the music of the fiddle, music for drinking and dancing. Women's music was domestic music, God's music, the music of the dulcimer and the autoharp, music for home, hearth, and church passed down from mother to daughter, from grandmother to granddaughter, from generation to generation.

As Buffwack and Oermann have shown, women's music often lamented mountain women's double marginalization.[1]

---

[1] Mary A. Bufwack and Robert K. Oermann, *Finding Her Voice: The Illustrated History of Women in Country Music* (New York: Henry Holt and Company, 1993).

Stand by Your Man and Your Daughters Shall Prophesy

As members of the class of rural poor, mountain women were relatively powerless in society at large. As women, they were powerless in their own homes and communities. Marriage, more often than not in the early teen years, meant the drudgery of backbreaking household labor and relentless, life-threatening childbearing. In the late nineteenth and early twentieth centuries, mountain women who were fortunate enough to survive childbirth often died of old age while in their forties. Songs like "Barbara Allen" and "Single Girl, Married Girl" expressed these women's efforts to come to terms with their low estate. The "old songs" women shared among themselves were their way of keeping hope alive.

Some of the more prominent women of country music are direct descendants of these Appalachian women's musical practices. As a child in the mountains of Tennessee, Dolly Parton learned the musical traditions of her foremothers and kept these alive in her own music. One of country music's finest songwriters, Dolly's best songs are perfect examples of the Appalachian primitive style. In 1987, Dolly teamed with EmmyLou Harris and Linda Ronstadt on the landmark *Trio* album, reviving and preserving the music of Dolly's mountain foremothers. Harris, who came into country music from the "hippie" folk side, and Ronstadt, who's career has traversed the boundaries between country and rock and, more recently, between country and mariachi, both viewed Parton as the genuine article—a native product of the musical traditions they had adopted.

In 1993, Parton teamed in another trio with Tammy Wynette and Loretta Lynn to record *Honky Tonk Angels*, an album that embodies the best of women's country music as it moved into the public sphere. Lynn, like Parton, also grew up among the poorest of the poor in remote Appalachia and learned music from her grandmother. In addition, like many of her mountain foremothers, Lynn was married and mother to large brood of children before she reached the age of twenty. Lynn's music combines Appalachian women's anguish with the forthrightness of the honky-tonk movement, resulting in a groundbreaking candor in giving voice to women's experience. Wynette grew up poor in rural Mississippi and became the first of country music's "show queens" by giving voice to the perspectives of the working-class women who have made up the lion's share of country music's audience.

The *Honky Tonk Angels* album begins with a cover of Kitty Wells' classic hit, "It Wasn't God Who Made Honky-Tonk Angels," on which Wells, the first "Queen of Country Music," makes a guest appearance. This song, like its provocateur Hank Thompson's "The Wild Side of Life," raises the question of the moral responsibility for broken relationships in an explicitly theological frame of reference. While Wells and Thompson disagree on whether the guilty party is the particular woman accused by Thompson or men in general as indicted by Wells, both absolve God of the crime. I like to think that Hank Williams's doctrine of providence—"When God made me, he made a ramblin' man"—is more honest. But the crucial point is that the question is raised *theologically*.

Discussing the women of country music as feminist theologians is no small task, especially given country music's reputation for traditionalism. Most female country artists would no doubt bristle at being called "feminist" and deny the accuracy of the charge—whether or not their music reflects feminist values. In part, feminist country artists' resistance to being labeled "feminist" is another case in point to the charge often raised by non-white women thinkers that mainstream "feminism" is out of touch with the concerns of poor and working-class women. The same resistance also reflects a fear of alienating country music's core audience by offending their traditional values.

In her book *Ladies First: Women in Music Videos*, Robin Roberts examines the ways some female artists—including some country artists—have exploited the medium of music video to voice "feminist messages." A feminist message, according to Roberts, is one that exposes and criticizes some aspect of women's oppression.[2] My task here is to examine feminist *theological* messages in country music. So, if I were to adopt Roberts's suggestion of what makes a message feminist and combine it with my explanation in chapter 1 of what makes a message theological, then my task would be to find country performances that expose and criticize some aspect of women's oppression by construing it in relation to God or to that which is of ultimate concern. Women artists' rejection of sexual double standards are often grounded, like Hank's hillbilly humanism, in a Christian-based understanding that all people are equal before God.

But feminist theologians generally seek to do more than merely expose and criticize women's oppression. Feminist theologians point out that, because men's voices have defined the terms and boundaries of the theological traditions, the theologies that have been constructed reflect men's ways of thinking. Feminist theologians contend that women's experiences must be recovered as a primary source or starting point for theological reflection if theology is going to be

---

[2] Robin Roberts, *Ladies First: Women in Music Videos* (Jackson: University Press of Mississippi, 1996) xxiii.

relevant to women's lives. Moreover, feminist theologians, like their secular counterparts, tend to emphasize the importance of solidarity or community among women. On both these counts, feminist theologians can find among women country artists true allies—allies so true, in fact, that their openness to women's experience extends in some ways beyond that of upper-middle-class academic feminists. As Roberts concludes her discussion of women artists in country music: "By celebrating their female solidarity, they reach a segment of the population that has been neglected by mainstream feminists."[3] Among the messages we will receive from women country artists is that the answers to ultimate questions—the meanings of life—are to be found within the mundane experiences of women.

Buffwack and Oermann suggest that the musical practices of those poor and working-class women who kept traditions alive by passing down the old songs from generation to generation represent the deepest roots of country music's heritage. As country music emerged as a commercial form and during the successive growth of the country music industry, the music continued to express working-class sensitivities. Honky-tonk music became "the voice of the loneliness, alienation, and loss of community in industrial mass society," and the dialectic embodied in the Hank Thompson/Kitty Wells exchange emerged: "Women were blamed as men expressed their feelings of victimization; but the culture responded with the women's point of view, and the argument about who victimized whom became institutionalized in the country sound."[4] So, from the outset,

---

[3] Ibid., 136.
[4] Buffwack and Oermann, *Finding Her Voice,* x–xi.

and even as the culture of commercial country music sought to impose traditional values, feminist messages have been present in country music.

But commercial country music has been mostly a man's world. Most of the artists were (and still are) men, as were (and are) the vast majority of music industry executives, producers, and other persons in positions of influence. Women artists never received top billing. Until fairly recently, an unwritten rule in country radio was that two songs by women artists should not be played back to back. Moreover, women artists were expected to fit in by conforming to standards of acceptable femininity. The three artists featured on the *Honky Tonk Angels* project were pioneers for women in country music. Examining their work will provide an opportunity to explore the ways in which country music has given voice to women's experience and how that experience has been construed theologically.

The Female Hank Williams

The artist who best exemplifies the emergence of honky-tonk feminism is Loretta Lynn. As the quote at the head of this chapter indicates, Lynn is ambivalent at best about her role as an advocate of feminist values. But the content and effect of the messages in her songs cannot be denied.

Loretta Webb, born in 1935, was raised among the poorest of the poor in a remote corner of Appalachia—Butcher Holler, Kentucky, to be exact—and learned music from her mother and grandmother the way Appalachian women did throughout the nineteenth and early twentieth centuries. At age thirteen, she married Oliver "Doolittle" "Mooney" Lynn. By age eighteen, she had four children, and

Mooney sought to escape Appalachian poverty by moving the family to Custer, Washington, where he would work in the timber industry. Mooney recognized Loretta's musical talent and pushed her to perform and write songs.

After winning a local talent contest and performing on a Tacoma TV broadcast, Loretta was noticed by timber industry magnate Norm Burley, who financed a recording trip to Los Angeles. Loretta recorded "Honky Tonk Girl" and became the first artist on Burley's new label, Zero Records. Loretta and Mooney loaded all the records in the back of their car and set out on a cross-country, grassroots marketing campaign, visiting every country radio station they could find and asking the disk jockeys to play Loretta's record. Their diligence paid off: "Honky Tonk Girl" reached number fourteen on the *Billboard* chart, and Loretta soon signed with Decca Records in Nashville. The rest, as they say, is history.

Loretta Lynn so transformed women's country music that producer Owen Bradley has called her "the female Hank Williams." Prior to Loretta, successful female artists remained within the confines of rather narrow models of femity. For example, Kitty Wells could sing of being done wrong by men, but her perspective and persona were those of the traditional housewife and mother. While Patsy Cline's off-stage and backstage brassiness is legendary, her torch-song repertoire is well within traditional feminine romantic bounds. But Loretta blows the roof off of traditional femininity. She issues ultimatums to her man in songs like "Your Squaw Is on the Warpath," "Don't Come Home A-Drinkin'(with Lovin' On Your Mind)," and her cover of Nancy Sinatra's hit "These Boots Are Made for Walking," and threatens female rivals in "Fist City," "You Ain't Woman

Enough (to Take My Man)," and "Woman of the World (Leave My World Alone)." Lynn has not shied away from exploring controversial social issues in her music. Her 1965 hit "Dear Uncle Sam" protests the Viet Nam War. In the 1971 "Rated X" she criticizes the sexual stereotyping of divorced women, while 1972's "The Pill" celebrates the liberating power of birth control. Buffwack and Oermann point out that Lynn's rise to stardom parallels the rise of the feminist movement. Lynn's "country-feminist point of view," in fact, represents a part of American culture ignored by mainstream media. Country music continued to be the voice of an alienated working-class, and the songs of Loretta Lynn and her successors chronicle the experience of women who must practice resistance not only at work, but also—and especially—at home.

Lynn herself recognizes that her songs broke new ground in portraying women's experience: "There's plenty of songs about how women should stand by their men and give them plenty of loving when they walk through the door, and that's fine. But what about the man's responsibility?" Lynn, in fact, rejects the view that women should be sole guardians of the moral order: "Well, shoot, I don't believe in double standards, where men can get away with things that women can't. In God's eyes, there's no double standard. That's one of the things I've been trying to say in my songs."[5] It was Lynn's honesty and candor that paved the way for later women artists who would continue to challenge traditional ways of viewing men and women.

---

[5] Loretta Lynn with George Vecsey, *Coal Miner's Daughter* (New York: Da Capo Press, 1996) 55.

In Loretta Lynn, we see the emergence in country music of a new level of feminist sensitivity. But what makes Lynn's honky-tonk feminism theological? In Appalachian musical traditions, the sacred and the secular are often intertwined or at least connected like pieces of a patchwork quilt. The repertoire of the Carter Family, who emerged from Ralph Peer's legendary Bristol sessions to become one of commercial country music's first star acts, included both gospel and secular songs, along with sentimental songs that blurred the distinction between the two. Dolly Parton carries on the tradition of blending the sacred and secular in her Appalachian primitive songs, such as "Appalachian Memories" and "Coat of Many Colors."

Lynn's music seems to come from some place other than her Appalachian heritage. She began her career on the West coast, where Bakersfield was the capital of country music. Lynn announces her musical identity in her first single, "I'm a Honky Tonk Girl," and her music is honky-tonk through and through. Aside from her autobiographical hit, "Coal Miner's Daughter," her music makes little explicit reference to her Appalachian past—and religion is notably absent from that song's catalog of childhood memories. Granted, like most country stars of earlier generations, Lynn has recorded albums of gospel songs. While one of these—*Who Says God is Dead?*—represents a rather clever and timely response to the radical theology movement of the 1960s, the bulk of Lynn's gospel material consists of cliché-ridden standards. Gospel albums by country artists tend to stand out as anomalies—like Christmas albums—uninfluenced by and unrelated to the artist's main body of work. Besides, as Spencer indicates, the deepest theological reflection is to be found in music that relates the struggles of everyday life to ultimate questions, whether or not that music happens to be explicitly religious.

In Lynn's music, as in the blues and in the music of Hank Williams or George Jones, the realm of male-female relationships is elevated to ultimate significance and serves as a crucible in which one's life can be transformed for good or ill. Over and again, Lynn sings of the devastating effects of infidelity: failed relationships are not trivial affairs, but represent the loss of one's whole world. The ultimate significance of the romantic relationship provides a framework for the social criticism in Lynn's more controversial songs.

In "Dear Uncle Sam," for example, the Viet Nam War effort is treated almost as if it were the protagonist's sweetheart's other woman. "You said you really need him," Lynn sings, addressing Uncle Sam, "but you don't need him like I do." Her man "proudly wears the colors of the old red, white and blue," she continues, "while I wear a heartache since he left me for you." The song's appeal depends on the listener's ability to relate to a situation where the loss of a loved one means the loss of everything—in other words, the situation of people who, as James Cone puts it in lines I quoted at the head of chapter 1, "possess little that is their own."

Similarly, several of Lynn's songs raise ultimate questions regarding a woman's reproductive health. Songs like "One's on the Way" and "Pregnant Again" recall the oppressive effects of childbearing—especially the ways pregnancy functioned to maintain male dominance to life-threatening degrees in the Appalachian communities where women's "sad songs" were preserved to become the core of country music's heritage.[6] Against this backdrop, one understands that reproductive freedom is indeed worth celebrating in "The Pill" as "too good to be real"—particularly when we remember that Lynn, like so many of her mountain foremothers, was raising a litter of several children while yet in her teens.

Lynn sings a message of working-class pride, evident in songs like "You're Lookin' at Country" and the autobiographical "Coal Miner's Daughter," that is consistent with what I outlined in chapter 2 as country music's core moral outlook, the "hillbilly humanism" of Hank Williams. As noted in chapter 2, Hank's hillbilly humanism starts from a Christian-based affirmation of the equal dignity of all persons regardless of social class, which is in constant tension with the lived awareness of social inequality. Lynn's songs of working-class pride offer a criticism of upper-class values similar to that found in Hank Williams's music. For example, in the aforementioned "One's on the Way," written for Lynn by Shel Silverstien, the life of a poor woman is specifically contrasted with the lifestyles of glamorous wealthy celebrities such as Jacquelin Kennedy Onassis. Lynn's early hit "Success" bemoans the negative effects that an obsession with wealth can have on a relationship.

Lynn's humanism is more complete and explicit than Hank's in that she raises her voice in specific affirmation of the equal dignity of women. Buffwack and Oermann see as one of Lynn's major contributions her making visible the plight of working-class women, who, shackled by the demands of day-to-day survival, do not have the same experience and concerns as upper-class feminists. In Lynn's

---

[6] See Buffwack and Oermann, *Finding Her Voice*, 2–23.

music, women stand up to their men, to other women, and to social forces that threaten their relationships.⁷ In addition to her message of female self-assertiveness, Lynn also sings of those traditional women's longings that seem to frustrate mainstream feminists. For example, in "Blue-Eyed Kentucky Girl," Lynn expresses a longing to give up the life of a world traveler so that she can be with "my babies at home." While much feminist writing has viewed motherhood as something that women need to be liberated *from*, this song posits motherhood as something to be liberated *for*. But isn't the desire to be responsible in one's relationships rather than accrue objective material accomplishments consistent with what Carol Gilligan and others have outlined as women's modes of moral reasoning? Isn't the desire to be freed from the constraints of a male-dominated industry in order to choose one's own ends consistent with feminist ideals of liberation? At any rate, this desire for freedom to fully actualize one's closest relationships is at the heart of what women's country music posits as working women's ultimate concern.

Lynn's advocacy for the marginalized includes other groups as well. Lynn, who describes herself as "one quarter Cherokee," has made efforts to champion the cause of Native Americans. Because of her pride in her Native American heritage, Lynn learned deconstruction when deconstruction wasn't cool: "I've also read some history books about my Indians to find out what the white man did. I've got white history books and red history books—and let me tell you. Friend, they tell different stories about the same events."⁸ She

---

⁷ Ibid., 312–14.
⁸ Lynn, *Coal Miner's Daughter*, 28.

also rejects the racism often associated with country music culture. In 1972, when Charley Pride was scheduled to present an award for which Lynn was nominated, she was advised not to show too much affection for him if she won, lest she offend bigoted fans and promoters who might cancel her shows. The advice angered her, in part because of principle and in part because Pride was a dear friend. She did win and, ignoring her advisors, gave Pride "a big old hug and a kiss right on camera" during the televised award show.

That Lynn's rejection of hierarchical distinctions among persons is rooted in theological sources is evident in her response when criticized for referring to president Nixon by his first name: "They called Jesus Jesus, didn't they?"[9] Lynn's own religious background sheds little light on her convictions. She never had a strong connection to organized religion and was not baptized until 1972. Her religious practice continues to be a curious amalgam of common-sense Christianity and mountain superstitions that sometimes resemble New Age spirituality. "Coming from the mountains," she recalls, "I have kind of funny beliefs anyway—kind of a mixture of religion and superstition. I know people in the Church of Christ ain't supposed to believe in reincarnation and seances and stuff, but I guess I do."[10]

But Lynn's music embodies convictions consistent with those of feminist theologians who emphasize women's experience as a primary source for theological reflection. In a 1972 essay titled "The Spiritual Revolution: Women's Liberation as Theological Re-Education," for example, Mary Daly suggests that "faith" be understood as "openness to

---

[9] Ibid., 158.
[10] Ibid., 169.

experience and ultimate concern."[11] Loretta Lynn's music is notable for its openness in voicing previously taboo aspects of working-class women's experience and for its efficacy in construing women's experience in relation to ultimate concern.

The music of Loretta Lynn conveys a message of hope absent from the music of Hank Williams and George Jones. Williams and Jones are preoccupied with death; Lynn sings about life. From her songs about birth to her pleas for the rebirth of romance, Lynn's music is about the possibility for a better tomorrow. A woman strong enough to confront her unfaithful man is strong enough to demand and achieve positive change. Her personal life bears out her dogged sense of hope: despite problems along the way, including his unfaithfulness and violent temper, she and Doolittle stayed with each other and made the best of their life together.

Standing By Your Man as a Feminist Act

In her music, Tammy Wynette wallows in the depths of working women's misery the way her one-time husband and duet partner George Jones and his predecessor Hank Williams had mined the pits of unmitigated male malaise. Wynette's own background is typical of the working-class women who make up the lion's share of country music's core audience and whose experience mainstream feminists are often accused of ignoring. Wynette was a hairdresser and single mother prior to becoming a singer. Early in her career,

---

[11] Mary Daly, "The Spiritual Revolution: Women's Liberation as Theological Re-Education," in *Feminist Theological Ethics*, edited by Lois K. Daly (Louisville: Wesminster John Knox Press, 1994) 129.

she found herself in a series of frustrating and abusive marriages, most notably her much publicized dramatic union with George Jones. Her music reflects her understanding of a world in which women who often have very little cling to unfulfilling romantic relationships in desperate hope for better days.

Wynette knows the frustrations faced by working-class women, and she gives voice to these frustrations in her music. Her legendary hit, "Stand By Your Man," is a song not about marital bliss, but of desperate resignation, the cry of a woman who feels she has no choice but to stay with her man no matter what. Wynette is at her low-down, gut-wrenching best when describing heartache from a child's perspective in songs like "D-I-V-O-R-C-E," "I Don't Wanna Play House," "Kids (Say the Darnedest Things)," and "Bedtime Story," perfecting the image of the heartbroken child used so effectively by Jones in the haunting "A Picture of Me Without You."

While Wynette may plumb the depths of working women's misery a bit more deeply than does Loretta Lynn, she does not roll over and die there. In her first top-ten single, "Your Good Girl's Gonna Go Bad," the frustration of working-class existence has reached a desperate boiling point. But the song responds to such desperation by rejecting sexual double standards much the way Lynn does in her music. Wynette's "good girl" claims the same prerogatives that men have traditionally enjoyed in country music culture. Also like Lynn, Wynette sings explicitly about working-class pride. She celebrates the pleasures of working-class life in her duet with Jones, "We're Not the Jet Set," which pokes fun at those who are. And like Lynn, she sings of those feminine longings usually considered anti-feminist. In "Dear

Daughters," she recounts the pain of separation from her children resulting from the traveling lifestyle of a performer. Wynette's music explores the extremes of working-class women's experience, from the depths of misery to the most exuberant of celebrations. Perhaps the highest of her celebratory tones is reached in her biggest and strangest hit: her 1992 performance on British group KLF's international techno-dance hit "Justified and Ancient," which topped pop charts in eighteen nations. The bacchanal "Justified and Ancient" video, in which Wynette appears, could be nothing less than shocking to country fans enamored of the traditional values she has represented.

But Wynette, like Hank and Jones, never left behind her rural, working-class roots. Ironically, Wynette followed "Justified and Ancient" by hosting a Southern Gospel Music program on TNN. At Wynette's memorial service, Dolly Parton reported that during a recent visit with Tammy, Wynette stated that she still had her cosmetology license. When she played a waitress on the CBS soap opera *Capitol* in 1986, she was portraying the kind of working-class woman with whom her music is most closely identified.

Even more than Lynn, Wynette has advocated causes in her music and in other arenas that trouble mainstream feminists. A mainstream feminist might point to Wynette as an example of a woman so conditioned by patriarchal mythology that she pursues her own liberation only on terms prescribed by the dominant mythology (such as the Cinderella myth—that a woman needs a man to rescue her). This paternalistic attitude (can feminists be *pa*ternalistic?) is reflected in Hilary Clinton's offensive reference to Wynette (for which she later apologized) at the first public intimations of President Bill Clinton's sexual indiscretions during the1992 presidential campaign.

Any casual dismissal of Wynette's message(s), however, ignores the fact that her music resonates with the experience of poor and working class women. For women who have little or no hold on any kind of economic security, romantic relationships easily become a matter of ultimate concern. A lower middle-class woman with marginal education and job skills is as likely to find her Prince Charming as she is to land a high-paying position that will provide a good life for her and her children. As Wynette's own relationships testify, romance can be a source of ultimate threat or a place where one finds the deepest satisfaction. By comparing the dismal reality of working-class romance with the mythical ideal, Wynette's music exposes the real conditions with which poor and working-class women contend.

I Like My Feminism a Little on the Trashy Side

The casual observer may think Dolly Parton an unusual candidate for feminist icon. Parton's unrelenting emphasis on physical appearance seems to embrace the very social pressures that feminism seeks to remove from women. Parton's bustline has been a popular topic of on-stage humor for a generation, a characteristic by which feminists and others wish popular culture would cease judging women. On the other hand, feminists ought to be able to applaud the fact that Parton has exercised almost absolute control over her image—even if it is not an image most feminists would choose—as well as over other aspects of her career.

Like Lynn, Parton has expressed ambivalence about being labeled feminist or aligned with specifically feminist causes. In a 1978 *Playboy* interview, when asked if she supported the Equal Rights Amendment, she evasively claimed that she was unable to "keep up with it." In another interview, she quips, "I had my own opinion long before women's liberation," implying that the women's movement was not relevant to her life. However, because Parton's career has crossed farther from country music culture into mainstream pop culture, her relationship to mainstream feminism is more complex and involved than that of either Lynn or Wynette. In a 1991 appearance on the *Tonight Show* during the week of Mother's Day, Parton introduced her song, "Eagle When She Flies" as follows: "I wanted to do a song for all the mamas out there. This is a song I actually wrote about my own mother, and about myself—about people like Mother Teresa, Amelia Earhart, Harriet Tubman, Eleanor Roosevelt, Anne Richards, and all the great women who've helped make this world more wonderful. I hope maybe you guys will appreciate this, too."[12] In this introduction, Parton begins with a nod to traditional family values, praising motherhood in general and her own mother in particular (a frequent theme for Parton). She sneaks in an autobiographical reference to her own larger-than-life aspirations, then aligns herself with feminist heroes from history, and closes with a statement of her own ebullient optimism: what makes all these women great is that they've made the world "more wonderful."

With such a hodgepodge of values and commitments, it is no wonder that an episode of television's *Designing*

---

[12] All three quotes are in Pamela Wilson, "Mountains of Contradiction: Gender, Class, and Region in the Star Image of Dolly Parton," *South Atlantic Quarterly* 94/1 (Winter 1995): 128.

Women portrayed Parton's empire as a glitzy but down-home alternative to the women's movement. Parton's music and career embody a set of values consistent with but also transcending the "hillbilly humanism" outlined earlier as country music's moral/theological core. The values Parton espouses can be discussed under the headings of traditionalism, humanism, community, and optimism.

Parton's traditionalism is seen not only in her praise of motherhood—a vocation which she herself has not followed—but also in her musical style. Parton's more traditional songs, such as "Coat of Many Colors" and "My Tennessee Mountain Home," would fit perfectly in a collection of nineteenth- and early twentieth-century Appalachian folk tunes. The lyrics of these songs also convey messages reflecting traditional values. "Coat of Many Colors" teaches that love and family are more valuable than material wealth. "My Tennessee Mountain Home," "Applejack," and "Appalachian Memories" affirm the value of local community.

With her 1998 album, *Hungry Again*, Parton returns to her traditional roots. She explains that she returned home and spent several weeks in "prayer and fasting" before writing the songs for *Hungry Again*. She also recorded the album in her hometown, co-producing it with her cousin, using her cousin's band as musicians. The resulting album features understated performances of exquisitely written songs reflecting a range of traditional styles—from bluegrass to gospel to honky-tonk.

Hungry Again's first single, "Honky-Tonk Songs," demonstrates Parton's fluency in that particular traditional country music style and also communicates the scope of her humanism. "Why don't more women sing honky-tonk songs?" Parton asks in the song's signature line. Women suffer misery as much as men, and at the hands of men—so why don't they sing about it as much as men? Here is another rejection of sexual double standards and an assertion of sexual equality: women's experience is equally as important as men's. In the above-mentioned *Playboy* interview, after avoiding a specific commitment to the ERA cause, Parton confessed her belief that "Everbody should be free: if you don't want to stay home, get out and do somethin'; if you want to stay home, stay home and be happy."

This is hillbilly humanism in a nutshell: everyone is equally valuable, regardless of class or gender. The Christian underpinnings of this message in Parton's music are even clearer than in Hank's. In "Coat of Many Colors," the biblical story of Joseph provides a metaphor of God's care interwoven with a dirt-poor mother's love for her little girl. In the autobiographical "Appalachian Memories," the family maintains hope through an ill-fated migration North to find factory work by "depending on our Jesus." On the *Hungry Again* album, "Honky Tonk Songs" appears alongside gospel numbers "Shine On," recorded in the church that Parton's grandfather once pastored, and "When Jesus Comes Calling for Me."

Parton's humanism is seen also in her anti-elitism. When she quips, "It costs a lot of money to look this trashy," she indicates her rejection of the elitist aesthetics of the affluent upper class. She embraces styles that the cultural mainstream, influenced by elitist aesthetics, find to be in poor taste: big hair, too much make-up, gaudy colors—the same types of styles that Elvis embraced and enshrined at Graceland. The allegedly "tacky" styles of the "Not-So-Rich-and-Famous" (to quote the Tracy Byrd hit) also have their day in the sun.

Parton has also championed the cause of the downtrodden in her movies. *Nine to Five*, in which she made her acting debut, farcically exposes the plight of female office workers in a patriarchal corporate culture and even raises the issue of sexual harassment before it was widely recognized as a serious issue. The movie's title song, which Parton wrote and performed, became an anthem for overworked, underpaid, working-class women. In *Rhinestone*, Parton plays a nightclub country singer, held captive by her contract with an unscrupulous promoter, who teams with a New York cab driver (played by Sylvester Stallone) to gain her liberation. Here, working-class determination and ingenuity cross regional cultural boundaries and prove victorious over capitalist greed. And in *Straight Talk*, down-home sincerity and honesty finally win out over a web of deceit spun by the stratagems and schemes of a corporate marketing machine.

Parton's commitment to community is also seen in her movies, music, and other enterprises. I see no reason to doubt her sincerity in claiming that one of her aims in opening her Dollywood theme park was to help her local community by bringing economic development to her home county. Rural sociologists might argue that the type of economic development that has ensued is not the best for preserving rural communities, but we can at least view Parton's intentions as consistent with her values. Parton's movies betray a wish for transplanting the bonds of community celebrated in songs like "My Tennessee Mountain Home," "Applejack," and "Appalachian Memories" to a wider environment. In *Nine to Five* and *Rhinestone*, solidarity among working-class characters from different backgrounds proves to be the key to fighting oppression.

Stand by Your Man and
Your Daughters Shall Prophesy

Parton's quest for community is not unlike the popular feminist ideal of "sisterhood." In *Nine to Five*, after all, it is three women who band together to undo the shackles of a patriarchal corporate culture. In "Honky-Tonk Songs," Parton's protagonist listens to Williams, Haggard, and Jones on the jukebox while she drowns her misery. While she finds some resonance with these male expressions of heartache, she longs for voices with which she can more closely identify. She seeks sisters in misery who will sing a blues that's more like her blues: "Why don't more women sing honky-tonk songs?" And, as "Coat of Many Colors" suggests, Parton sees the bonds of community among women as rooted in Christian/biblical tradition and passed down matrilineally.

Where Parton diverges from the general outlook we've seen in country artists is in her optimism. While Hank Williams, George Jones, and Tammy Wynette expand their realism into a fatalism that wallows in the misery of life and sees little hope for redemption, Parton responds to adversity with renewed determination to overcome. Her optimism is evident throughout her musical repertoire, from the exuberance of "Tennessee Homesick Blues" to the quiet satisfaction of "My Tennessee Mountain Home," from the joyful anticipation of "Rockin' Years" to the steadfast determination of "Starting Over Again" and "Appalachian Memories." In "Coat of Many Colors," the taunts of classmates cannot undo or even shake the self-respect instilled in the song's young protagonist by her mother's love.

Even when Parton explores the downside of life and love, as in "Jolene" and "Here You Come Again," she does not sound defeated. Responding to a question about Whitney Houston's version of the melancholy "I'll Always Love

You," which Parton wrote about her painful break from Porter Wagoner, she responds: "Who would have thought that little old simple song could have done all that? I'm very proud of her, I'm very proud of the song, and I'm very proud for me that I made all that money out of a little heartbreak."[13] At times, Parton has taken her optimism to bizarre extremes, as in her mercurial cover of Don Fransisco's triumphant contemporary gospel standard, "He's Alive," and her own triumphant celebration of an aspect of women's experience seldom set to music, "PMS Blues."

Parton's optimism can be seen as a de-eschatologizing of the gospel song tradition's postponement of Christian hope into the afterlife. For Parton, hope is a here and now reality. With a firm belief in herself and her dreams, grounded in the love she received from her family and in whatever quirk of nature causes some creative geniuses to be ambitious enough to make their dreams come true, Parton has risen from abject poverty to become queen consort of a large financial empire. Perhaps most significantly, she has done so while retaining control over her own image. She has followed *Hungry Again* by delving deeper into her roots in two Grammy-winning bluegrass albums. Dolly Parton has been who she wants to be. In her music, she communicates her conviction that anyone can do the same.

Can Honky-Tonk Angels Fly?

Fast-forwarding to the present, as country music redefines itself in the post-Garthian age, women are more

---

[13] From Paul Kingsbury, "One-on-one with Dolly Parton," *Journal of Country Music* 19/2 (1997): 32-33.

prominent than ever and continue to sing ever more directly about women's experience. Perhaps it is instructive that the five artist photos on the cover of the mass market edition of Lawrence Leamer's chronicle of country music in the 1990s, *Three Cords and the Truth*, are of four women and only one man. The unwritten radio rule about not playing two songs by women back to back is long gone. Music by women artists has become as bold and raucous and sensual as the music of men was in the heyday of honky-tonk.

The medium of music video has been one vehicle for the growth in women artist's popularity. But video is a two-edged sword. While it increases the visibility of artists and their messages, it favors artists who conform to popular ideals of beauty and encourages visual images of sexual objectification. What is one to make, for example, of the contradictions in the coupling of Shania Twain's vocal message of monogamy and male responsibility with her visual images of titillating sensuality? Or of Mindy McReady's in-your-face rejection of sexual double standards in "Guys Do It" sung to male viewers ogling her bare midriff?

Roberts argues that overtly sexual visual images of women are not necessarily anti-feminist. Sexuality, after all, is one potential source or locus of power for women. In many music videos—as in many films, TV commercials, and other visual images—the portrayal of women's sexuality does promote a view of women as objects intended solely for the use and pleasure of men. But, as Roberts suggests, music videos can also portray women's sexuality in ways that counter the dominant tendency toward objectification: "Some feminist music videos deal with sexuality in a forthright, nonjudgmental, and entertaining fashion. By depicting sexuality as something that women have a right to express and control, these music videos contradict the stereotypical and limited depiction of women's bodies in other music videos."[14] Thus, videos like those of Twain and McReady can be seen as portraying women in control of their own sexuality.

Certainly, the message of women's right to sexual self-determination does not reach all audience members with equal clarity. While female fans (with whom Twain especially has struck a chord) may celebrate and identify with Shania Twain's sexual freedom and assertiveness, male viewers who watch her videos are more likely to experience arousal than conscientization. That sexuality remains problematic in country music culture is evident in Twain's response to questions about the sensuality in her videos. Initially, Twain sought to deny that her image had anything to do with sex, explaining it in terms like health or energy, much the same way Conway Twitty had denied that his double-entendre laden songs were really about sex a generation earlier. And John Derek, one of the chief architects of Twain's image, is not known as an opponent of the sexual objectification of women.

However, the evolution of Twain's career seems to support an interpretation similar to that suggested by Roberts. Twain's rise to superstardom may have been fueled by the titillating images in her most popular early videos, such as "Any Man of Mine," "The Woman in Me," and "You Win My Love." But her focus seems to have shifted once she reached the plateau. The last single released from her *The Woman in Me* album was "This Little Child," a song about

---

[14] Roberts, *Ladies First*, 64–65.

social justice. And the first singles and videos from her more recent *Come On Over* album seemed to display a move away from making direct appeals to male sexual desire. For example, the video of "Still the One," which was aired on MTV as well as the country networks, serves the "eye candy" to female rather than male viewers by featuring the towel-wrapped hips and glistening bare torso of a male model. The video of "Honey I'm Home" features Twain in a highly energetic but not sexually provocative concert scene, while the song's lyrics convey a feminist message by highlighting women's experience and rejecting sexual double standards. "Honey I'm Home" catalogs the uniquely feminine details of the female protagonist's hard day at work, including references to panty-lines and PMS. But she finds consolation at home, where she expects her mate to "bring me a cold one" and take care of the domestic chores while she rests and unwinds.

In "That Don't Impress Me," Twain returned to the formula that launched her massive popularity—lyrics expressing female self-determination combined with highly sexual visual images. Her next release, "Man, I Feel Like a Woman," is perhaps the most titillating of her videos to date, featuring a strip tease motif in which Twain replaces her customary bare midriff with bare thighs and cleavage. Even the lyrics to this song specifically reject the compulsion to "act politically correct." Yet the video is also a wicked satire of Robert Palmer's "Addicted to Love" and "Simply Irresistible" videos. Twain's video replaces the gyrating spandex-clad women in Palmer's videos with gyrating, spandex-clad male models. Twain's male models mimic the poses, dance moves, and suggestive gestures of the female models in Palmer's earlier videos, betraying a subversive feminist message on the part of Twain's video producer. Country music culture does retain a good deal of its ambivalence about sex and about what is appropriate for women, necessitating strenuous efforts at image control by artists and their management teams. Twain continues to have to defend her image. In a September 1998 *TV Guide* interview, she states: "I always try to explain to people that it's not about sex. Sensuality is part of being feminine. If you feel that you want wear something that's sexy, that doesn't mean that you're looking for sex."[15] But, as attested by the fact that Twain's rise to stardom rode an image so sensual that it needs explaining, the boundaries have become drastically more open for women. After all, Dolly Parton's "PMS Blues" appears on her 1994 *Heartsongs* album and would not have been likely to find a receptive audience earlier in her career. Finally, women can sing about any topic they wish with as much openness as is available to men.

For example, Nashville native and Loretta Lynn sound-alike Deana Carter plaintively and concretely recalls her protagonist's first sexual encounter in her debut hit single, "Strawberry Wine." The song explores the struggle to understand what it means to become a woman and concludes with the conscientizing question, "Is it really him or the loss of my innocence I've been missing so much?" Carter's deeply honest feminist confession stands in stark contrast to the cynical humor and mock nostalgia in Garth Brooks's "That Summer," a prototypically male version of the adolescent rite of sexual passage, despite some ostensible

---

[15] From Mark Lasswell, "Country's Better Half," *TV Guide* 46/38 (19 September 1998): 20–31.

similarities in the two songs' uses of pastoral imagery. Moreover, the choice to title Carter's debut album after the humorously self-assertive cut "Did I Shave My Legs for This?" betrays a self-conscious effort to make a feminist statement. After all, the album's third single—"Count Me In"—would yield a much more logical title for a debut album.

Women artists have exercised their newfound freedom for explicitness to explore controversial social issues in song. Garth protégé Martina McBride tackles the issue of domestic violence in her hit, "Independence Day," which is perhaps the most profound feminist theological statement in country music. This song employs biblical, civil-religious, and apocalyptic imagery in telling the story of a woman who burns down her house with her abusive husband and presumably herself inside. The blend of imagery exposes how Christian myth and patriotic myth are conflated in patriarchal America to reinforce an arsenal of traditional "values" that often have damaging effects on women and children. The rhyming phrases "roll the stone away, let the guilty pay" together call the patriarchal powers and principalities to accountability not least by suggesting that the crucifixion of Jesus is an apt metaphor for the systemic crucifixion of women. The plaintive repetition of "roll the stone away" as the song begins to fade evokes a pentecostal prayer for an eschatological undoing of patriarchal domination. "Independence Day" is not McBride's only strong feminist statement: her number one hit, "A Broken Wing," tells the story of a woman's victory in gaining freedom from an emotionally abusive relationship. Her hit "God-Fearing Women" humorously portrays a woman's desperation to escape the oppressive limitations of small-town culture, including small-town church culture.

Lorrie Morgan, a second generation member of the Grand Ole Opry and candidate to become heir to Tammy Wynnette's throne as *grande dame* of country music, also sings of the passages in women's lives and vocalizes other feminist messages. Morgan was married to country singer Keith Whitley, who tragically followed in the tradition of Hank Williams in drinking himself to death. Perhaps her process of learning that his death was not her responsibility—of breaking the chains of co-dependency—played a role in empowering her to sing of female self-determination. One of Morgan's protagonists gives her man "Five Minutes" to discern how to satisfy her. Her "What Part of No Don't You Understand" gives all women the answer phrase for overbearing males. In "Watch Me," a woman challenges her incredulous lover's refusal to believe that she will really leave, while "I Didn't Know My Own Strength" offers a retrospective celebration of a woman's freedom from an unfulfilling relationship. Her two 1998 hits, "Go Away" and "One of Those Nights," assert a woman's sexual self-determination. "Something in Red" is a classic chronicle of the stages in a woman's life.

Reba McEntire awakens from the patient forbearance of "Whoever's In New England" to tackle similarly controversial concerns. She sings about a casual sexual encounter that results in HIV infection in her hit, "She Thinks His Name Was John." Reba also sounds a feminist note in "Is There Life Out There?"—a song whose protagonist bemoans her discontent and ponders the possibility of seeking fulfillment outside her roles as housewife and mother. But a comparison of the audio and video versions of "Is There Life Out There?" reveals an ambiguity about women's roles similar to that expressed by women artists of Lynn, Wynette, and Parton's generation. The song itself leaves the impression that the protagonist is considering leaving her family, an option that might not have rested well with country's more conservative listeners. In the song's video, however, Reba portrays a woman who goes back to school and completes her college degree with the help of her husband and children, finding in the process a deeper satisfaction within rather than beyond her family. Certainly the fact that the sound recording and the video played simultaneously in their respective venues offered conservative radio audiences an authoritative interpretation that allowed them to accept the song. But even the deradicalized video conveys a soft feminist message about the division of household labor by depicting the husband as taking on a larger portion of the domestic duties so that the wife can pursue her studies.

Another song in which a woman contemplates abandoning her long-held domestic role is Mary Chapin Carpenter's "He Thinks He'll Keep Her." In Carpenter's song, the woman *does* leave. And audiences continued to buy her records. Carpenter is an Ivy League folkie and avowed feminist who managed to creep into country music's big tent just as the 1990s boom was beginning and to find a receptive audience for her songs. Unlike, Reba, who has managed to survive the transition from the age of country's glamour queens to whatever the 1990s can be called, Carpenter had no previous generation of fans to lose. Her songs struck a chord with a newer, more sophisticated audience. Some older fans viewed her with the same contempt toward "outsiders" that a previous generation had heaped upon "folkies" Olivia Newton-John and John Denver.

But this time, leading artists did not campaign against the Mary-come-lately. Granted, the first verse of Alan

Jackson's sardonic hit, "Gone Country," is quite possibly aimed specifically at Carpenter. But Carpenter found a receptive audience among other artists as well as among fans. In fact, through its video, cut from the 1992 CBS television special "The Women of Country," Carpenter's "He Thinks He'll Keep Her" became sort of an anthem for the country-feminist vanguard of the 1990s. The video pictures a concert scene in which Carpenter is joined by a chorus of other female artists—Suzy Boggus, Kathy Mattea, Patty Loveless, Pam Tillis, Trisha Yearwood, and Emmylou Harris. The feminist ideal of sisterhood had come home—down home.

Boggus makes a feminist statement her own in "Hey Cinderella," which wryly subverts the Cinderella myth. Boggus's 1998 hit, "Nobody Love, Nobody Gets Hurt," a clever account of a failed convenience store robbery, features a strong and effective female protagonist. The female clerk notices the title's Freudian slip in the note written by the would-be robber and confronts him with the possibility that he doesn't really want to follow through with his plan, thus turning a situation of male aggression into a situation of mutual dialogue.

Tillis sings of female heroines who wade through the trials and travails of women in the 1990s. In "Seems Like All the Good Ones Are Gone," for example, Tillis's protagonist is a single career-woman who is beginning to sense the ticking of the proverbial biological clock. In "Betty's Got a Bass Boat," Tillis satirizes the common view that a woman's worth relies on her marrying a good man. Mattea, a hillbilly loyal to her home state of West Virginia, invades the conventionally male domain of fast cars with big engines in "455 Rocket" and includes some sassy sexual double entendre (*a la* Conway Twitty) to boot. Wynonna Judd similarly crosses gender expectations, making a sardonic feminist statement in "Girls with Guitars."

Patty Loveless has in many ways followed in her cousin Loretta Lynn's footsteps. Like Lynn, she is the daughter of a Kentucky hillbilly family. Like Lynn, she worked with the Wilburn Brothers early in her career. Like Lynn, she found her strongest musical influences outside her hillbilly roots (for Lynn, the West coast honky-tonk scene was predominant; for Loveless, it was the edgy country-rock sound of Linda Ronstadt). And like Lynn, she sings of women's experiences. But unlike Lynn, Loveless migrated with her family to the city while she was young, so her own life recreates the social dislocations that shaped the history of commercial country music. Loveless sings country music with a rock edge *a la* Linda Ronstadt. But she also sings poignantly about the trials and passages in a women's lives with 200 years of Appalachian anguish in her voice. In "How Can I Help You to Say Goodbye?" for example, she depicts how women help one another across the generations to deal with some of life's "necessary losses," to borrow Judith Viorst's term. In "You Don't Even Know Who I Am," a shuddering lament, a couple awakens to the mundane reality that their relationship has died.

Trisha Yearwood's first number one hit, the narrative ballad "She's In Love With the Boy" depicts assertive female characters who are willing to defy authority. Her duet with Garth Brooks, "Squeeze Me In," turns the tables on a conventional complaint about men who neglect their love lives by being overly involved in their careers. In the Brooks/Yearwood song, it is the woman who is on a professional fast-track, prompting complaints from her male love interest. Yearwood also makes a strong feminist statement in "Real Live Woman," whose lyrics portray the gaining of perspective by a woman who comes to the self-assuredness to define her own identity without being confined by societal expectations and pressures. The video for this song is set in a seedy looking, "peep-show" joint with a neon sign advertising "real live women." But as the curtains for each window open, the gawking male onlookers see women performing various family and professional roles instead of exotic dancers, giving the message that "real live women" are more interesting and exciting than the artificial, over-sexualized image of women so dominant in our hyper-mediated society.

Emmy Lou Harris's inclusion in the video, like her rise to prominence in mainstream country music, signals a dramatic but unnoticed shift in country music culture. As a member of the "hippie," "folk" avant-garde, Harris once represented the primary external threat to country music. But by the time of her inclusion in the "Women of Country" project, she had become president of the Country Music Foundation—the main organization charged with preserving country music's heritage. Harris's career has included all types of American folk and country music—including protest songs—so that her credentials as a champion of feminist and other progressive causes cannot be denied. The fact that she has become a standard-bearer for authentic country music belies an important fact: it is the music that matters above all else.

The female act that best embodies the new ideal of country womanhood is the Dixie Chicks. Because of the timing of their rise to fame and because the three of them were all (for the moment) blonde, the Dixie Chicks were superficially perceived as country music's version of the

Stand by Your Man and Your Daughters Shall Prophesy

Spice Girls. But the Dixie Chicks have actual musical talent. Sisters Emily Robison and Martie Maguire are accomplished bluegrass musicians who play banjo, fiddle, mandolin, and dobro on the Dixie Chicks' recordings and performances and provide the rich vocal harmonies endemic to the Dixie Chicks' unique sound. Lead vocalist Natalie Maines has arguably the best pipes in country music. Her performance on the Chicks' cover of "Stand By Your Man" on the *Tribute to Tradition* album is as good as Tammy Wynette's original. And, as if it were a small thing to match pipes with the queen of country music, Maines also equals rock goddess Stevie Nicks on the Dixie Chicks' brilliant, bluegrass-style cover of Fleetwood Mac's "Landslide."

Emily and Martie were part of an earlier configuration of the group that released three albums on independent record labels. But I will limit my discussion to the current configuration of the Dixie Chicks because this is the group that has risen to international superstardom in the post-Garthian era of country music. The trio's uniqueness is seen first in their fashion sense. Earlier generations of female country artists have tended to conform to some widely accepted sense of style. Kitty Wells dressed like a rural housewife. Patsy Cline wore cocktail dresses that matched her torch song repertoire. Then came the era of the show queens: from Tammy Wynette to Reba McEntire, female artists wore elaborate gowns and even featured multiple costume changes during a performance. At the other end of the spectrum, artists like EmmyLou Harris de-emphasized style by wearing blue jeans and other comfortable clothes. Then Shania Twain ushered in the era of the belly-button, in which female artists are supposed to look like pin-ups or pop divas. Dolly Parton was always in a class by herself, but even she sought to be stylishly tacky. The Dixie Chicks, on the other hand, have an eclectic fashion sense that can only be described as weird. They were named to Mr. Blackwell's Fortieth Anniversary "Worst Dressed Women List" in 2000 with the epithet: "They look like a trio of truckstop fashion tragedies trapped in a typhoon—some days a little bit wacky, but most of the time tacky, tacky, tacky."[16] With their couture, not to mention their vow to get chicken feet tattoos with every career milestone (number one singles or albums, gold or platinum albums), the Dixie Chicks declare their independence from narrowly constricting images of what women are supposed to look like.

The new Dixie Chicks' first two singles, "I Can Love You Better than That" and "There's Your Trouble," construct a sassier version of the traditional female country music posture of talking to a man about a female rival. Their hit, "Tonight the Heartache's On Me" is the perfect answer to Dolly Parton's plea for more women to sing honky-tonk songs, a honky-tonk lament with a walking bass line and some memorable lines that only a liberated woman could sing—"I wonder if he told her she's the best he's ever known, the way he told me every night when we were all alone." But it is the Dixie Chicks' most controversial single, "Goodbye Earl" that cements their place as the standard bearers of the new honky-tonk feminism. "Goodbye Earl" sets to music the simple plot of Fannie Flagg's *Fried Green Tomatoes*—two female friends conspire to murder one of the friends' abusive husband, and then live happily ever after. Though the song evinces a tongue-in-cheek attitude, many country radio

---

[16] "Mr. Blackwell's 40th Annual 'Worst Dressed Women List': A Veritable Symphony of Style-Free Flops," *Salon.com,* January 11, 2000.

stations were reluctant to play the single, on the premise that murder is not funny. Apparently, these stations' program directors did not read the disclaimer at the bottom of the printed lyrics in the CD liner notes: "The Dixie Chicks do not advocate premeditated murder, but love getting even."

But the hullabaloo over Garth's "The Thunder Rolls" had already opened the video airwaves to controversial subject matter. The star-studded "Goodbye Earl" video, featuring TV actors Dennis Franz (*NYPD Blue*) as Earl and Lauren Holly (*Chicago Hope*) and Jane Krakowski (*Ally McBeal*) as Mary Anne and Wanda, the song's two female protagonists, became a monster hit and won the 2000 CMA Video of the Year Award. The video adds to the tongue-in-cheek attitude of the song by having the dead and decomposing Earl dance in the grand finale scene. It goes without saying that finding humor in the murder of a wife-beater makes a rather bold feminist statement. Another song from the Chicks' *Fly* CD has fomented a different type of controversy. The Dixie Chicks have been sued by the heirs of gospel writer and publisher Albert E. Brumley for incorporating part of the chorus of Brumley's "Ill Fly Away" into their raucous song, "Sin Wagon"—a song in which Maines extols the virtues of "mattress dancing." "Sin Wagon" is a rather extreme example of what Robin Roberts sees as a woman controlling and asserting her own sexuality.

All of these artists have several things in common. First, they continue to demonstrate that the basic equality of all persons posited in Hank's hillbilly humanism implies the rejection of sexual inequalities and double standards. Second, they show that life's meaning is revealed in life's simplest moments—the necessary losses, the small joys, and the daily struggles for survival and hope. Third, they show the ultimate importance of community among women. Fourth, they assert to varying degrees a woman's right to self-determination.

The new country ideal of womanhood is apparently beginning to trickle down to male artists. Sammy Kershaw sympathizes with the travails of working women in "National Working Woman's Holiday." Collin Raye preaches against the objectification of women in "I Think about You." Certainly the old messages about women as men's toys continues to be heard—in songs like Little Texas's "God Bless Texas" and Toby Keith's "A Little Less Talk and a Lot More Action." But such messages now are balanced by the recognition of women's independence in other songs.

The new ideal is captured in Chad Brock's "Evangeline," ironically a song in which a male protagonist celebrates a young woman's beauty. The heroine of this song is a college student who works for the summer at her Papaw's store on the lake. An anonymous cast of "the boys" hangs around nearby just to see her—enchanted by the sight of her bronze shoulders against her tank top and the way she walks along the dock in her flip-flops. Each of these boys "would love to say 'that girl's mine.'" But Evangeline does not belong to any of them—how could such a woman deign to belong to some anonymous boy who cannot see deeply enough to value anything beyond physical appearances. Nor does she belong to her Papaw (the only other named character in the song), who is resigned to the fact that he must soon get along without her. Evangeline belongs to herself. She pursues her own values, not the shallow values of these anonymous "boys" who would aspire to possess her. She values work, unlike the boys who wile away their leisure watching her. She values education: she will soon return to school—Louisiana

State University one infers from the song's geography—where she is preparing for a life she chooses. Is she studying to be a lawyer, a doctor, an engineer? The song does not tell us. But the song does makes clear that she is on a higher plane than the lakeside culture that makes up the song's setting. She is literally *evangeline*, bearer of good news. She is a feminine emanation of the gospel. She is a gift from God, an angel perhaps, hovering above these anonymous locals and vacationers for a season, offering them a glimpse of her glory, then returning to her world and her own values. The gospel she embodies among them is the gospel of female self-determination. One hopes they will get the message.

"I will pour out my spirit on all flesh, and your sons *and your daughters* shall prophesy," predicted the prophet Joel and Peter at Pentecost. More recently, Paul Simon and Art Garfunkel noted that "the words of the prophets are written on the subway walls and tenement halls." Still more recently, Mary Buffwack and Bob Oermann chronicle the story of women in country music as a story of a woman *Finding Her Voice*. Well, the daughters have found their voices, and they have become prophets, prophesying not with "Sounds of Silence," but with loud honky-tonk sounds. As Roberts concludes, women artists in the 1990s have been "selling to the huge country audience the message that women's subordination is unacceptable and that strong, powerful female voices can and will be heard."[17]

---

[17] Roberts, *Ladies First*, 137.

Epilogue

All I Really Need to Know I Learned from Country Music

"That other song is the one my daddy likes. It's about 'everybody needs somebody to love,' and God is love, so it seems like to me that it's a song about God. If God is love. Because its about God and the Bible says God is love."[1]
—from *Killer Diller* by Clyde Edgerton

We have now traveled through the history and culture of country music and noted some of the major themes expressed in the messages of country songs—from Hank Williams's hillbilly humanism to Dolly Parton's honky-tonk feminism.

---

[1] Clyde Edgerton, *Killer Diller* (New York: Ballantine Books, 1991) 188.

We have considered how country music's dialectical movement in and out of the cultural mainstream has brought shifts in emphasis as the message changes with the target audience. We have seen that women in country music have hoed a slightly different row than their male counterparts. But we have also seen that a core style and message remains constant.

This core message—what I call country music's moral/theological outlook—includes and expands the emphases of Hank Williams's hillbilly humanism. Recall that we described theology as articulating the assumptions that shape one's view of the world. The assumptions that comprise country music's moral/theological outlook can be clustered around several overlapping themes. These themes include dignity, fate, love, work, responsibility, and hope.

Dignity

In chapter 2, we saw that Hank Williams's "hillbilly humanism" begins with an affirmation of human dignity. In songs like "Men With Broken Hearts" and "Pictures from Life's Other Side," Hank specifically urges compassion for those who are down and out. Hank's critique of wealth and protests at the injustice of life are rooted in this fundamental conviction of human dignity.

Human dignity implies equality. Hank's "common people" are just as good and honorable as anyone else. The many songs asserting working-class pride, such as Merle Haggard's "Working Man Blues," Alabama's "Forty Hour Week," and Aaron Tippin's "Working Man's Ph.D." and "I Got It Honest," are protests against a stratified status system

All I really Need to Know I Learned from Country Music

in which those with greater wealth, style, and leisure are more highly regarded than others.

Even during country music's crossover swings into the cultural mainstream, this fundamental affirmation of human dignity remains strong. Garth Brooks celebrates the worth of country music's traditional working-class audience in songs like "Friends in Low Places," "American Honky-Tonk Bar Association," and "Two of a Kind Working on a Full House." In other songs, and in the messages communicated by the visual images in his videos, Garth expands the message of human dignity. The lyrics to "We Shall Be Free" are primarily a call for racial equality, but also include pleas for greater tolerance with respect to religion and sexual preference. The video for "The Dance" features images of Martin Luther King, Jr., among others, again reinforcing the need to fight for racial justice. The "Standing Outside the Fire" video features a Special Olympics competition, calling attention to the dignity of the mentally disabled. The "Thunder Rolls" video calls attention to the plight of battered women. Garth's most recent single, "Love is Thicker than Blood," issues a call for peacemaking in a world torn by war and terror because "We're all sons and daughters of something that means so much more."

The women of country music, as we saw in chapter 4, have expanded the message of human dignity to include the equal dignity of women. From Kitty Wells and Loretta Lynn to Mindy McReady and Shania Twain, female country artists have questioned and rejected sexual double standards. Female artists including Twain, Trisha Yearwood, and Dolly Parton have explicitly asserted women's right to define their own identity and values. Tammy Wynette's songs, like the music of the Appalachian women to whom female country music traces its roots, lament the double marginalization of poor and working-class women.

For Hank Williams and Dolly Parton, this affirmation of the dignity of persons is rooted specifically in Christian theological understandings. Hank's agonizing lifelong struggle with faith reveals that he found in Christianity enough truth to challenge and inspire him, but not enough to save him. Dolly Parton had the opposite experience. For her, the Christianity of her parents and grandparents was a comfortable quilt on which to rest and add as she explored her own spirituality. That country music's fundamental conviction of human dignity and equality is rooted in Christian tradition poses at least a double irony here.

It is ironic, first, that the Christian churches and denominations most closely associated with country music's cultural context—the rural South—have been bastions of social stratification along the lines of race, class, and gender. Can it be that Loretta Lynn understands a core biblical principle better than the leaders of the Southern Baptist Convention do? Of course, as we have seen, neither have the institutions and culture of country music always embodied the equal dignity of all persons that is expressed poetically in country songs. This should not surprise us. Few peoples actually live up to their highest ideals. The seed of liberation that led to the abolition of slavery lay dormant in Christian tradition for 1,800 years before it found concrete expression in human history. Likewise, the scope of the principles of liberty and equality espoused by classic liberal political thought and expressed in the United States' Declaration of Independence has unfolded over time to include an ever-widening assemblage of persons.

The second irony inherent in the Christian origins of country music's humanistic outlook is that country music rejects the other-worldly solace that Christian tradition (especially popular Christian music) espouses as the answer to the lived contradiction between human dignity and socioeconomic marginalization. We have seen that heaven functions in Hank Williams's corpus of songs merely as an end to suffering, not a recompense for it. While religion may provide the insight that all people are equal in God's sight, religion apparently fails to provide an adequate prescription for the inequality experienced by those who are "looking up from the bottom."

A few artists may get their humanism from non-Christian sources. Mary Chapin Carpenter, for example, is influenced by "secular" feminism. Most country artists derive their belief in the equal dignity of all persons from a homogenized blend of a number of elements, including Christian theology, American populism, and country music tradition.

Fate

Country music's affirmation of basic human dignity stands in tension with the lived experience of marginalization. The primary way country music accounts for this marginalization is through a belief in fate. Country music recognizes that our lives are often driven by forces or powers greater than us, over which we have little or no control. Hank Williams claims, "When God made me, he made a ramblin' man." George Strait and Garth Brooks have both had hits with songs in which the rodeo's mystical hold on a cowboy functions as a metaphor for ultimate power. Most often, romantic love functions as the metaphor for the power or powers that control life.

Scott Peck's longtime best-selling book *The Road Less Traveled* begins with the simple, three-word sentence, "Life is difficult."[2] Country music also proceeds from a fundamental awareness that life is disconcertingly difficult, unpredictable, beyond human control, and unfair. Simply and most obviously, country music rejects the illusion that life is supposed to be easy. Country music is realistic. As Lynn Anderson sings, "I beg your pardon, I never promised you a rose garden."

In "I'll Never Get Out Of This World Alive," Hank expresses country music's core fatalism with humor and directness: "Now you're lookin' at a man that's getting' kinda mad/ I had lots of luck but it's all been bad/ No matter how I struggle and strive/ I'll never get out of this world alive."

The fate that dooms romantic relationships in Hank Williams's songs reflects a general sense that the powers determining life's direction are capricious and beyond control. Again, with romantic love as a metaphor for ultimate power, Hank sings "I can't help it if I'm still in love with you." Similarly, in "You Win Again," heartache is seen as inevitable: "This heart of mine could never see / what everybody saw but me/ Just trusting you was my great sin / What can I do? You win again."In the concluding verse to "I'll Never Get Out Of This World Alive," Hank presents fate as all-encompassing: "I'm not gonna worry wrinkles in my brow/ 'Cause nothin's ever gonna be all right no how/ No

---

[2] M. Scott Peck, *The Road Less Traveled: A New Psychology of Love, Traditional Values, and Spiritual Growth* (New York: Simon & Schuster, 1978) 15.

matter how I struggle and strive/ I'll never get out of this world alive."

Fate is capricious. The "Pictures From Life's Other Side" to which Hank draws our attention just happen—sometimes they can be traced to bad decisions, but sometimes they can't. "In "Men With Broken Hearts," Hank urges listeners to feel compassion and empathy toward the less-fortunate, because "the God that made you made them too." The wooden cigar-store Indian "Kawliga" represents us all, powerless to control our destiny in face of the inexorable forces that determine life's direction.

Other artists share Hank's fatalism. In "Then What," Clay Walker warns that adultery leads to a situation in which "fate can't wait to kick you in the butt," this attributing to fate an element of justice similar to that found in Hank's warning that "Your cheatin' heart will tell on you." But the majority view in country music seems to emphasize fate's capriciousness and uncontrollability. As Mark Chesnutt complains, "Every time I make my mark, somebody paints the wall."

Country music, then, expresses an awareness that life is ultimately beyond our control. We become aware, as theologian James Gustafson puts it, of "powers that sustain us and bear down on us." Sometimes, the powers that bear down on us appear stronger than the powers that sustain us.[3]

---

[3] James Gustafson, *Ethics from a Theocentric Perspective*, Volume Two: Ethics and Theology (Chicago: University of Chicago Press, 1984) 207-209.

Responsibility

In spite of its awareness of the capriciousness of fate, country music nonetheless emphasizes human moral responsibility. In the world of country music, actions have consequences. Despite the fact that humans are "born to trouble as the sparks fly upward" (Job 5:7), we are responsible for our choices. Responding to life's troubles by seeking escape in booze and sex only brings more trouble. One ends up, like George Jones, "still doing time in a honky-tonk prison."

Though life is often unfair and is ultimately beyond control, one cannot escape the consequences of one's choices. Hank Williams promises, "Your cheatin' heart will tell on you." Conversely, Moe Bandy confesses, "I cheated me right out of you." George Jones adds, in a song that would make a fine valedictory to his career (but we all hope his career continues!), "I'm living and dying with the choices I've made." The humor with which country music presents themes of adultery and alcohol abuse is usually a bitter irony—these are seen as the negative consequences of bad choices. Drinking and cheating represent a failure to carry out a fitting response to the difficulties one faces in life.

Garth Brooks's optimism arises specifically from this recognition that choices have consequences despite the fact that life is beyond control. If we live in a damned-if-you-do, damned-if-you-don't kind of world, then we might as well eke out all the enjoyment we can from the relationships and opportunities we have. A lost love, then, is an occasion to be grateful that it was good while it lasted and to celebrate with "Friends in Low Places" rather than drown one's sorrows in lonely isolation. As Willie Nelson put it, "I'd rather be sorry for something I've done than for something that I didn't do."

If Pablo Cruise had been a country band, I would quote their song "Rainbows Colored in Blue," which observes, "There's two ways of looking at the holes in your shoes—you can dig the ventilation, or you can sing the blues." But since Pablo Cruise was not a country band, I'll quote the Bible instead. As Qoheleth puts it,

> Go, eat your bread with enjoyment, and drink your wine with a merry heart; for God has long ago approved what you do. Let your garments always be white; do not let oil be lacking on your head. Enjoy life with the wife whom you love, all the days of your vain life that are given you under the sun, because that is your portion in life and in your toil at which you toil under the sun. Whatever your hand finds to do, do with your might; for there is no work or thought or knowledge or wisdom in Sheol, to which you are going (Eccl 9:7-10).

When the powers that bear down on us seem stronger than the powers that sustain us, we can respond in different ways. We can curse our fate and try some escapist maneuver (in country music, escapism takes the form of booze, sex, or death). Or we can make the best of it and move on with our lives.

Simplicity

One fitting response to life's difficulties is to find pleasure in simple things. The superiority of simple living is a frequent theme in country music. If country music is indeed a musical form associated with economically marginalized folk, then it should contain some critique of wealth. Hank Williams makes clear that "Wealth Won't Save Your Soul" and criticizes the relentless pursuit of money in many songs. He laments the fate of someone living in a "loveless mansion on the hill." In "House of Gold," Hank states that amassing wealth amounts to denying God and dooming one's soul to eternal torment: "I'd rather be in a cold, dark grave, and know that my poor soul is saved,/ Than to live this life in a house of gold, and deny my God, and doom my soul." Country music arises first and foremost from an existential awareness of the difficulty of life and stands in sharp contrast to the overly optimistic messages of other popular culture texts. Hank Williams focuses our attention on "Pictures from Life's Other Side."

Other artists have followed Hank in criticizing wealth. Sometimes, the critique of wealth is bitter. Merle Haggard's "If We Make It Through December" chronicles the tragic effects of poverty on family life. Harlan Howard's "Busted" is another bitter lament of poverty. Hank Snow's "Saginaw, Michigan" combines a bitter critique of the pretensions of the wealthy with an ironic turnaround by which the song's working-class protagonist gains the upper hand. More recently, Alan Jackson bemoans the effects of the global economy on small-town community in "The Little Man." Travis Tritt, in "Lord Have Mercy on the Working Man," raises the specter of economic injustice by asking, "Why the rich man does the dancing while the poor man pays the band."

Often, the critique of wealth takes the form of a celebration of simpler living. In one of her many hits, Loretta

Lynn proudly proclaims, "If you're looking at me, you're looking at country," while her signature song celebrates the simple joys of life as a "Coal Miner's Daughter." Many of Dolly Parton's songs express joy amid the hardships of Appalachian poverty. More recent artists also celebrate the superiority of rural simplicity in songs like Tracy Byrd's "I'm From the Country (and I Like It That Way)," Tim McGraw's "Country Boys and Girls Gettin' Down on the Farm," Travis Tritt's clever play on words in "Country Club" and Montgomery-Gentry's "Daddy Won't Sell the Farm." Another way country music asserts the superiority of simpler living is by proclaiming working-class pride as seen in songs I've already mentioned, such as Aaron Tippin's "I Got It Honest" and "Working Man's Ph.D.," Brooks and Dunn's "Hard Working Man," and Alabama's "Forty Hour Week." A more reflective note is struck in Confederate Railroad's "Daddy Never Was the Cadillac Kind," a song in which retrospective wisdom reveals that Daddy's working-class values surpass the superficial, glitzy materialism of the current generation. A similar message is expressed in Tritt's "Where Corn Don't Grow."

Sometimes, the celebration of simple living adopts an ironic pose reminiscent of Jeff Foxworthy's redneck jokes. Randy Travis prefers the company of "A Better Class of Losers" rather than the highbrow crowd his social-climbing mate prefers. Tracy Byrd parodies television's celebration of wealth in "Lifestyles of the Not So Rich and Famous," and Joe Diffie exploits a redneck stereotype in "Pickup Man." Sammy Kershaw worships "The Queen of My Double-Wide Trailer," while the Bellamy Brothers simply plead, "Gimme a, gimme a, gimme a redneck girl."

It all adds up to the fundamental conviction that a person's value has nothing to do with money or its trappings. The country blues standard "Ain't Gonna Worry My Mind" sets these priorities: "Got no money in my pocket / Can't get rich working overtime/ But as long as you can't buy the springtime in Virginia/ I ain't gonna worry my mind."

The underlying affirmation of the equal dignity of all persons regardless of social class forms the core of country music's hillbilly humanist moral/theological outlook, and provides the basis for a tradition of social criticism from the perspective of the white working class. Even Garth Brooks recognizes that one needs "Friends in Low Places."

Love

As we have seen, it is love that serves most often as a metaphor for ultimate power. In country music, romantic love functions as a metaphor for salvation, and lost love as a metaphor of damnation. Love holds the power to redeem or to destroy—the power of life and death. Indeed, as George Strait sings, "If you ain't loving, then you ain't living."

Put most simply, life is better if you have someone to love. The country blues standard "Ain't Gonna Worry My Mind" is again relevant: "Love is all that ever makes you happy if the truth be told/ Moonlight's been my only silver and the sun my only gold. Here, love is credited with the power to bring happiness, as well as to compensate for lack of material wealth. Familial love also adds meaning to life, or at least provides some balm against life's troubles. In the tradition of Mother songs, the prison-bound protagonist of one of Confederate Railroad's hits takes comfort in the knowledge that "Jesus and Mama always loved me." Dolly

All I really Need to Know I Learned from Country Music

Parton celebrates the love of family in many of her songs. The catalog of responses to the 11 September 2001 tragedy in Alan Jackson's thoughtful "Where Were You" culminates with, "Or did you just stay home and cling tight to your family/ Thank God you had somebody to love." Even the love of a pet can make a positive difference. Hence, Tom T. Hall observes, "There ain't but three things in this world that's worth a solitary dime, and that's old dogs, and children, and watermelon wine."

But something as powerful as love is not always benign. Country music's deepest roots reach into ballads like "Barbara Allen" and "Knoxville Girl"—songs in which love kills. Love is dangerous and uncontrollable. Hank Williams says, "I Can't Help It (If I'm Still in Love With You)." On the other hand, George Strait sings, "You Can't Make a Heart Love Somebody." Love is its own power, over which mere mortals are powerless. As Kenny Rogers sings, "Something's got a hold on me/ It's cheap but it ain't free/ Love or something like it's got a hold on me."

One day my two daughters were arguing about the Dixie Chicks' song, "Cowboy Take Me Away." My younger daughter was convinced that it is a song about God. My older daughter said it's just about love. When they asked me who was right (given that I am a renowned expert on both country music and God), I said they both were. "Dad!" they exclaimed in unison. I know that they did not like my answer because they pronounced "Dad" with three syllables. A two syllable "Dad" signals mild annoyance. Three syllables means you've really blown it. But a song about love *is* a song about God, as I've suggested throughout this book, and as Clyde Edgerton's mentally challenged character proclaims in the quote at the head of this chapter.

In country music, as in the music of any marginalized group, love is ultimate power. As I quoted James Cone in an earlier chapter, "People who have not been oppressed physically cannot know the power inherent in bodily expressions of love.... In a world where a people possess little that is their own, human relationships are placed at a premium. The love between men and women becomes immediate and real."[4] It is desperate love that keeps Tammy Wynette standing by her man despite his flaws and empowers Loretta Lynn to challenge a female rival in "Fist City." It is overwhelming but unrequited love that drives Hank Williams to despair in "You Win Again" and "Cold, Cold Heart."

Hope

Despite its realism, fatalism, and frequent pessimism, country music is an expression of hope. Country music embodies hope precisely because it is *music*. The very fact that one can raise one's voice to sing about life's difficulties helps to ameliorate those difficulties. As George Strait sings, "If It Weren't For Country Music I'd Go Crazy." Music is a fundamental human response to the emotions that accompany the passages of life. Country music gives specific attention to life's passages, and it self-referentially identifies itself as a balm in Gilead for many of life's woes.

In his hit "Luckenback, Texas," Waylon Jennings clearly identifies music's power to heal: "There ain't but two things in life that make it worth livin/ That's guitars that tune good and firm feelin' women/ Now I don't need my name in the

---

[4] James Cone, *The Spirituals and the Blues* (Maryknoll, NY: Orbis, 1992), pp. 114-115

All I really Need to Know I Learned from Country Music

marquee lights/ 'cause I got my song and I got you with me tonight." Here, music is portrayed as equal to romantic love in having the power to "make life worth livin'." The song's chorus highlight's music's anesthetic function: "Between Hank Williams pain songs, and Dewberry's train songs, and 'Blue Eyes Crying in the Rain'/ Out in Luckenback Texas, ain't nobody feeling no pain." Good country songs—especially, "pain songs"—have the effect, ironically, of relieving pain. Setting one's pessimism to music becomes a kind of optimism. Country music functions like the Psalms of lament, providing a framework for raising or deepening misery and despair to the level of ultimate concern and then releasing them.

Again and again, country music represents itself as tonic for the downhearted. Alan Jackson is clear that country is the only kind of music that works for heartache: "Don't rock the jukebox—I want to hear some Jones." Dolly Parton pleads for more women to sing honky-tonk songs, and the Dixie Chicks oblige with "Tonight, the Heartache's on Me." In the most desperate moments, Merle Haggard prays, "Sing Me Back Home." Joe Diffie says the afterlife can wait as long as there is country music to listen to in "Prop Me Up Beside the Jukebox When I Die."

Hank Williams is reported to have adapted a line from "I'll Never Get Out of This World Alive" into a sort of benediction he pronounced at his concerts: "Don't worry about nothin' 'cause it ain't gonna be alright nohow." Yet, the fact that Hank can sing and joke about it means that it's alright if it ain't alright. The overall message of country music echoes the ethos of the blues in saying that as long as we can sing about it, it will be alright. The title of one of

Patty Loveless's hits captures this cathartic effect of country music: "You Can Feel Bad If It Makes You Feel Better."

Despite its fatalism, country music participates in the blues' hope that things will get better—or that if things don't get better, we can learn to live with it. There is relief available for life's suffering. Beer, whiskey, and tequila offer one type of relief—"Ten Rounds with Jose Cuervo" will ease anyone's pain for a while. Illicit sex offers another temporary relief—now and then a person may need someone to "Help Me Make It through the Night." Love offers the promise of a more lasting cure for life's troubles. Love, of course, doesn't always work out. When love goes wrong, the situation may be even more painful than before.

But even the heartache of love gone wrong can be eased. One's "friends in low places" are always available to party along and help drown a memory. The kingdom of heaven is a honky-tonk. And there's no cover charge.

Bibliography

Abrahams, Roger D. and George Foss. *Anglo-American Folksong Style*. Englewood Cliffs NJ: Prentice-Hall, 1968.

Allen, Bob. Review of *I Lived to Tell It All* by George Jones with Tom Carter. *Journal of Country Music* 18/3 (1996): 41–43.

Berry, Wendell. *Sex, Economy, Freedom & Community*. New York: Pantheon, 1992.

Blaser, Kent. "'Pictures from Life's Other Side': Hank Williams, Country Music, and Popular Culture in America." *South Atlantic Quarterly* 84 (1985): 12–26.

Bruce, Dickson D., Jr. *And They All Sang Hallelujah: Plain-Folk Camp-Meeting Religion, 1800–1845*. Knoxville: University of Tennessee Press, 1974.

Bufwack, Mary A. and Robert K. Oermann. *Finding Her Voice: The Illustrated History of Women in Country Music*. New York: Henry Holt and Company, 1993.

Byrd, James Preston, Jr. "The Slave Spiritual as Apocalyptic Discourse." *Perspectives in Religious Studies* 19 (Summer 1992): 199–201, 204–16.

Campbell, Will D. "The World of the Redneck." *Katallagate: Journal of the Committee of Southern Churchmen* 5 (Spring 1974): 34–40.

———. "Elvis Presley as Redneck." *Baptist Peacemaker* 15 (Fall–Winter 1995): 1–2.

Cassels, Louis. *What's the Difference? A Comparison of the Faiths Men Live By.* New York: Doubleday and Company, 1965 (reprinted at www.religion-online.org).

Clarke, Leslie L. and Michael K. Miller. "The Character and Prospects of Rural Community Health and Medical Care." In *American Rural Communities*, edited by A. E. Luloff and Louis E. Swanson. Boulder: Westview Press, 1990.

Cone, James H. *The Spirituals and the Blues.* New York: Seabury Press, 1972; reprinted Maryknoll, NY: Orbis Books, 1992.

Cushman-Wood, Darren. "Redneck Liberation Theology: Recovering a Radical Gospel for White, Working-Class Evangelicals." *The Other Side* 28 (October 1992): 46–49.

Cusic, Don. *The Sound of Light: A History of Gospel Music.* Bowling Green OH: Bowling Green State University Popular Press, 1990.

Cusic, Don, editor. *Hank Williams: The Complete Lyrics.* New York: St. Martins, 1993.

Dickinson, Chris. "Garth in the Park: Do You Recall What Was Revealed?" *Journal of Country Music* 20/1 (1999): 10-17.

Dunne, Michael. *Metapop: Self-Referentiality in Contemporary American Popular Culture.* Jackson: University Press of Mississippi, 1992.

Edgerton, Clyde. *Killer Diller.* New York: Ballantine Books, 1991.

Ellison, Curtis W. *Country Music Culture: From Hard Times to Heaven.* Jackson: University Press of Mississippi, 1995.

Escott, Colin. *Hank Williams: The Biography.* New York: Little, Brown & Company, 1995.

Feiler, Bruce. *Dreaming Out Loud: Garth Brooks, Wynonna Judd, Wade Hayes, and the Changing Face of Nashville.* New York: Avon Books, 1998.

Feiler, Bruce. "Gone Country: The Voice of Suburban America," *New Republic* 214/6 (5 February 1996): 19–24.

Fillingim, David. "The Cheatin' Song: A Redneck Blues." *West Texas Historical Association Year Book* (1995): 106-117.

———. "A Flight from Liminality: 'Home' in Country and Gospel Music." *Studies in Popular Culture* 20/1 (October 1997): 75–82.

———. "The Gospel Songs and the Cheatin' Songs: Redneck Theological Discourse and the Problem of Suffering." *Studies in Popular Culture* 19/2 (October 1996): 185–95.

———. "Music Stretching to the Heavens." *Seabreeze: The Guide to Coastal Living* 1 (September/October 1986): 20–21.

Fiorenza, Elisabeth Schüssler. *Revelation: Vision of a Just World.* Minneapolis: Fortress Press, 1991.

Flippo, Chet. *Your Cheatin' Heart: A Biography of Hank Williams.* New York: St. Martin's, 1981.

Foxworthy, Jeff. *You Might Be A Redneck If...* Atlanta: Longstreet, 1989.

———. *Red Ain't Dead: 150 More Ways to Tell If You're a Redneck.* Atlanta: Longstreet Press, 1991.

———. *Check Your Neck: More of You Might Be A Redneck If...* Atlanta: Longstreet Press, 1992.

Friedman, Kinky. *Road Kill.* New York: Simon & Schuster, 1997.

Goddu, Teresa. "Bloody Daggers and Lonesome Graveyards: The Gothic and Country Music." *South Atlantic Quarterly* 94/1 (Winter 1995): 57–80.

Goff, James R. *Close Harmony: A History of Southern Gospel.* Chapel Hill: University of North Carolina Press, 2002.

Goodson, Steve. "Hillbilly Humanist: Hank Williams and the Southern White Working Class." *Alabama Review* 46 (April 1993): 105–36.

Greenway, John. "Country-Western: The Music of America." *The American West* 5 (November 1968): 32–41.

Gustafson, James N. *Ethics from a Theocentric Perspective.* Volume Two: Ethics and Theology. Chicago: University of Chicago Press, 1984.

Halberstadt, Alex. "Merle Haggard." *Salon.com* (November 14, 2000).

Jacoby, Susan. *Wild Justice: The Evolution of Revenge.* New York: Harper & Row, 1983.

Jennings, Waylon, with Lenny Kaye. *Waylon: An Autobiography.* New York: Warner, 1996.

Jones, George, with Tom Carter. *I Lived To Tell It All.* New York: Villard, 1996.

Keillor, Garrison. *WLT: A Radio Romance*. New York: Viking, 1991.

Kingsbury, Paul. "One-on-one with Dolly Parton." *Journal of Country Music* 19/2 (1997): 31-37.

Lasswell, Mark. "Coutry's Better Half." *TV Guide* 46/38 (19 September 1998): 20–31.

Leamer, Lawrence. *Three Chords and the Truth: Behind the Scenes with Those Who Make and Shape Country Music*. New York: HarperPaperbacks, 1997.

Ledbetter, Mark. "An Apocalypse of Race and Gender: Body Violence and Forming Identity in Toni Morrison's *Beloved*." In *Picturing Cultural Values in Postmodern America*, edited by William G. Doty. Tuscaloosa: University of Alabama Press, 1995.

Lewis, George H., editor. *All That Glitters: Country Music in America*. Bowling Green: Bowling Green State University Popular Press, 1993.

Lynn, Loretta, with George Vecsey. *Coal Miner's Daughter*. New York: Warner Books, 1976; reprinted New York: Da Capo Press, 1996.

"Mr. Blackwell's 40th Annual 'Worst Dressed Women List': A Veritable Symphony of Style-Free Flops," *Salon.com*, January 11, 2000.

Malone, Bill C. *Singing Cowboys and Musical Mountaineers: Southern Culture and the Roots of Country Music*. Athens: University of Georgia Press, 1993.

———. *Country Music USA*. Austin: University of Texas Press, 1985.

———. "Honky Tonk: The Music of the Southern Working Class." In *Folk Music and Modern Sound*, edited by William Ferris and Mary L. Hart. Jackson: University Press of Mississippi, 1982.

Metress, Christopher. "Sing Me a Song about Ramblin' Man: Visions and Revisions of Hank Williams in Country Music." *South Atlantic Quarterly* 94/1 (Winter 1995): 7–27.

Moore, Mary Elizabeth Mullino. *Teaching From the Heart: Theology and Educational Method*. Minneapolis: Fortress Press, 1991.

O'Meilia, Matt. *Garth Brooks: The Road Out of Santa Fe*. Norman: University of Oklahoma Press, 1997.

Peck, M. Scott. *The Road Less Traveled: A New Psychology of Love, Traditional Values, and Spiritual Growth*. New York: Simon & Schuster, 1978.

Peterson, Richard A. *Creating Country Music: Fabricating Authenticity*. Chicago: University of Chicago Press, 1997.

Peterson, Richard A. "The Dialectic of Hard-Core and Soft-Shell Country Music." *South Atlantic Quarterly* 94/1 (Spring 1995): 273–300.

——— and Kern, Roger. "Hard-Core and Soft-Shell Country Fans." *Journal of Country Music* 17/1 (1995): 3–6.

Roberts, Robin. *Ladies First: Women in Music Videos*. Jackson: University Press of Mississippi, 1996.

Sample, Tex. *White Soul: Country Music, the Church, and Working Americans*. Nashville: Abingdon Press, 1996.

Sizer, Sandra S. *Gospel Hymns and Social Religion: The Rhetoric of Nineteenth-Century Revivalism*. Philadelphia: Temple University Press, 1978.

Smith, Stephen A. and Jimmie N. Rogers. "Saturday Night in Country Music: The Gospel According to Juke." *Southern Cultures* 1 (1995): 229–44.

Spencer, John Michael. "Overview of American Popular Music in a Theological Perspective." *Black Sacred Music* 8/1 (Spring 1994): 205–17.

Swanson, Louis E. "The Human Dimension of the Rural South in Crisis." In *The Rural South in Crisis: Challenges for the Future*, edited by Lionel J. Beaulieu. Boulder: Westview Press, 1988.

Talbert, Charles H. *The Apocalypse: A Reading of the Revelation of John*. Louisville: Westminster John Knox Press, 1994.

Tichi, Cecilia. *High Lonesome: The American Culture of Country Music*. Chapel Hill: University of North Carolina Press, 1994.

———, editor. *Readin' Country Music: Steel Guitars, Opry Stars, and Honky Tonk Bars*. Durham: Duke University Press, 1995.

Tinsley, Jim Bob. *For a Cowboy Has to Sing*. Orlando: University of Central Florida Press, 1993.

Tindal, George. "The Benighted South: Origins of a Modern Image." *Virginia Quarterly Review* 40 (Spring 1964): 281–94.

Tosches, Nick. *Country: The Biggest Music in America*. New York: Stein and Day, 1977.

———. "George Jones: The Grand Tour." In *The Country Reader: Twenty-five Years of the Journal of Country Music*, edited by Paul Kingsbury. Nashville: Country Music Foundation Press and Vanderbilt University Press, 1996.

Tunnell, Kenneth D. "Blood Marks the Spot Where Poor Ellen Was Found: Violent Crime in Bluegrass Music." *Popular Music and Society* 15 (Fall 1991): 95–115.

Vonnegut, Kurt. *Palm Sunday: An Autobiographical Collage*. New York: Delacorte, 1981.

Welwood, John. *Journey of the Heart: Intimate Relationships and the Path of Love*. New York: HarperPerennial, 1990.

"When Whites Migrate from the South." *US News & World Report* 55 (14 October 1963): 70–73.

Whisnant, David. "Gone Country: *High Lonesome* and the Politics of Writing about Country Music." *Journal of Country Music* 17/2 (1995): 62–66.

White, John I. *Git Along Little Doggies: Songs and Songmakers of the American West*. Urbana: University of Illinois Press, 1975.

Williams, Roger M. *Sing a Sad Song: The Life of Hank Williams*. Champaign: University of Illinois Press, 1981.

Yoder, John Howard. *When War is Unjust: Being Honest in Just War Thinking*. Minneapolis: Augsburg Publishing House, 1984.

Index

Acuff, Roy, 11, 34
African American music, 3, 4-5, 26, 31-32, 38, 49, 74, 92
Alabama, 142, 151
Allman Brothers, 77
Anderson, John, 25, 67,
Anderson, Lynn, 146
apocalyptic, 72-75, 82-88, 89-91; biblical, 72-74; in literature, 74-75, in country music, 82-88, 89-92; dualism, 89-91
Arata, Tony, 93
Atkins, Chet, 15
authenticity, 11-12, 64, 67, 81, 94-96, 97-98; of Southern Gospel Music, 28

Bandy, Moe, 35, 39, 43, 148
baptism, 55, 56, 114
Bare, Bobby, 83

Beatles, 71
Bellamy Brothers, 151
Berry, Wendell, 9
Blues, 4-5, 11, 25-26, 36, 40, 41, 49, 55, 56-57, 111, 155-156
Bluegrass, 4, 15
Boggus, Suzy, 132
Boston, 76
Bradley, Owen, 108
Bristol sessions, 9-10
Brock, Chad, 138
Brooks & Dunn, 151
Brooks, Garth, 12-13, 37, 67, 69-71, 75-82, 88-100 124, 128, 133, 135, 143, 145, 148, 152; as Chris Gaines, 97-99; authenticity of, 70, 80-82, 94-98; Central Park concert, 72; childhood, 76; education, 77; impact on country

music, 70-71, 80-82, 99-100; musical influences, 76-77; videos, 78-79, 89
Bruce, Dickson, 8
Brumley, Albert, 137
Bufwack, Mary A., 14, 18, 102, 106, 109, 112, 139
Byrd, Tracy, 67, 99, 100, 151

Campbell, Will, 7-8, 9, 28, 40
Carpenter, Mary Chapin, 131-132, 145
Carson, Fiddlin' John, 9, 10, 64
Carter, Deana, 128-129
Carter family, 9-10, 33, 58, 82, 83
Cash, Johnny, 18
Cassels, Louis, 6
Cheatin' songs, 23, 33-42, 48; history of, 33-35
Chesnee, Kenny, 99
Chesnutt, Mark, 36, 67, 147
Cinderella myth, 117-118, 132
Clark, Guy 83
class, working, 8-9, 19, 21, 28-29, 34, 50-51, 66, 104, 106, 109, 12, 116-118, 142-143
class, upper-middle, 67, 112
Cline, Patsy, 108, 135

Clinton, Hillary Rodham, 117-118
"Coal Miner's Daughter," 65, 151
Coe, David Allen, 58
Cone, James, 24, 25, 32, 34, 36, 38, 40, 41, 57, 111, 153-154
Confederate Railroad, 99, 151, 152
conscientization, 31, 126
cosmic cowboy movement, 83
Country Music scholarship 2, 13-14, 15-19, 55-56
Country radio, 13, 66, 67, 70, 76-77, 100, 107, 125
cowboy(s), 80-81, 82, 92-93
Curtis, Sonny, 38
Cusic, Don, 26, 40, 43

Dalhart, Vernon, 9, 10, 64
Daly, Mary, 114-115
"Dance, The," 80, 89, 93
Daniels, Charlie, 77
deconstruction, 26, 113
Denver, John 12, 76, 131
Diamond Rio 99
Dickens, Hazel, 24
Diffie, Joe, 67, 99, 151, 155
Disco, 12, 33
Dixie Chicks, 97, 134-137, 153, 155

Index

domestic violence, 78-79, 129, 136-137
Doobie Brothers, 77
Drinking, 35, 47, 55, 58, 62-63, 65, 89, 148, 156
Dunne, Michael, 88

Eagles, 76, 99
Ecclesiastes, 149
Edgerton, Clyde 141, 153
education, 78
Ellison, Curtis W., 3, 11, 57, 59, 60, 89
escapism, 41, 51, 148, 149

fatalism, 41, 42, 50, 53, 54, 60, 145-147, 148, 155
Feiler, Bruce, 76, 80, 81
feminism, 18, 19, 38, 104-106, 110, 112-113, 118-119, 145
feminist theology, 104-106, 110, 114-115
Fiorenza, Elizabeth Schüssler, 73
Flagg, Fannie, 136
Fleetwood Mac, 135
Flippo, Chet, 44, 48, 54, 64
Fogleberg, Dan, 76
Foley, Red, 76
folk music 10, 12, 33, 71, 76, 120, 131, 133
Foxworthy, Jeff, 7, 67, 151
Francisco, Don, 124

Fricke, Janie, 39
Friedman, Kinky, 21, 70
"Friends in Low Places," 78, 80, 152, 156

Gilligan Carol, 113
Goddu, Teresa, 29, 49, 83
Goodson, Steve, 49-52
gospel music, 36, 49, 92, 53-54
Grand Ole Opry, 46-47
Greenway, John, 37
Gustafson, James, 147

Haggard, Merle, 64-66, 84, 123, 142, 150, 155
Hall, Tom T., 21, 153
hardcore country music, 13, 15, 64
Harris, Emmylou 83, 132, 134, 135
Hayes, Kendall, 35
heaven, 29-33, 53-54, 57, 145
hillbilly, 1, 2, 10, 33-34
hillbilly gothic, 29, 49, 83
hillbilly humanism, 50, 112-113, 120-121, 137-138, 142, 152
home, 84, 103
"Home on the Range," 84
honky-tonk music, 2, 34, 36
Houston, Whitney, 123
Howard, Harlan, 21, 150

humanism, 5, 50, 112-113, 120-121, 137-138, 142, 152
Husky, Ferlin, 82

"I Saw the Light," 53, 54
"I'm So Lonesome I Could Cry," 55
infant mortality, 29
irony, 51, 63, 67, 148

Jackson, Alan, 4, 12, 15, 25, 58, 66, 67, 131-132, 150, 152-153, 155
Jennings, Waylon, 59, 77, 154
Jesus, 53-54, 58, 71, 83, 114, 129
Job, 148
Jones, George, 4, 59-62, 67, 77, 83, 89, 111, 115, 116, 123, 148, 155
Journal of Country Music 59, 72
Judd, Wynona 133
Judds, 83
justice, 37, 53, 147

Kafka, Franz, 59
Keillor, Garrison, 24, 34
Keith, Toby, 138
Kendalls, 4, 36
Kershaw, Sammy, 3, 67, 99, 138, 151

King, Larry, 79-80
King, Martin Luther, Jr., 8, 89, 143
King, Rodney, 92
Kiss, 76

Leamer, Lawrence, 14, 69, 76, 125
Lennon, John, 71
liberation theology, 26, 31, 41, 50
Little Texas, 138
"Long Gone Lonesome Blues," 54, 55
Louisiana Hayride, 46, 47
love, 3-4, 24, 48, 50, 60, 61, 85, 87, 90, 111, 115, 118, 123-124, 152-154, 156
Loveless, Patty, 4, 132, 133, 155
"Luckenbach, Texas," 154-155
Luke the Drifter, 49, 50, 98
Lynn, Loretta, 37, 65, 77, 101, 103-104, 107-115, 117, 128, 130, 133, 143, 150, 154
Lynryd Skynryd, 77

Malone, Bill, 10, 14, 81
Mandrell, Barbara, 12

Index

marginalization, 7-9, 52, 63, 102-103, 112-113, 144, 145, 149-150
Marshall Tucker Band, 77
Mattea, Kathy, 132
McBride, Martina, 78-79, 129
McCann, Lila, 100
McCoury, Dell, 4
McCurdy, Ed, 71
McDaniel, Mel, 4
McEntire, Reba, 2, 37, 130-131, 135
McGraw, Tim, 151
McLean, Don, 72
McReady, Mindy, 125, 143
Miller, Roger, 67
Montgomery-Gentry, 151
Moody-Sankey revivals, 27, 29
Morgan, Lorrie, 130
motherhood, 113, 119
murder ballads, 39, 83, 153
musicology, 21

Nashville Sound, 12, 81
Native Americans, 113
Nelson, Willie, 37, 77, 82, 83, 84-88, 148
New Age spirituality, 114
Newton, Juice, 25
Newton-John, Olivia, 12, 76, 131
Nicks, Stevie, 135

Nitty Gritty Dirt Band, 82, 95
Nixon, Richard, 114

Oak Ridge Boys, 82-83
O'Connor, Flannery, 44, 55, 56, 59
Oermann, Robert K., 14, 18, 102, 106, 109, 112, 139
"Okie from Muskogee," 65-66, 81
O'Meilia, Matt, 69-71, 76
Onassis, Jaqueline Kennedy, 112
optimism, 55, 123, 148, 154-155
outlaw movement, 77

Pablo Cruise, 149
Palmer, Robert, 127
Parton, Dolly, 18, 77, 83, 103-104, 110, 118-124, 128, 131, 135, 141, 143, 144, 151, 155
Payne, Rufus Tee-tot, 11, 34, 45
Pearl, Minnie, 54
Peck, M. Scott, 146
Peer, Ralph, 9-10
Peterson, Richard, 13, 15, 81
Pinn, Anthony, 4-5, 25
political correctness, 9, 19
politics, 66, 102, 117-118

poverty, 8, 24, 29, 50-51, 103
Presley, Elvis, 26-27, 71, 121
Pride, Charley, 114
protest, 36-37, 39, 41, 142

Qoheleth, 91, 149

racism, 66, 114, 143
radio, 13, 66, 67, 70, 76-77, 100, 107, 125
Raye, Collin, 83, 138
"Red-Headed Stranger," 84-88
rednecks, 7-9, 14, 28-29; defined, 7-9
Rich, Charlie, 11
Ricochet, 3
Rimes, LeAnn, 100
Roberts, Robin, 105-106, 125-126, 139
rock music, 76
Rodeheaver, Homer, 27
rodeo, 80-81, 95-96
Rodgers, Jimmie, 9-11, 34, 57
Rogers, Kenny, 37, 76, 153
Ronstadt, Linda, 83, 99, 103, 133
Rose, Fred, 46

salvation 3-4, 152
Sample, Tex, 14, 19, 41, 52, 66

Sankey, Ira, 27, 29
Seeger, Pete, 24
sex, 4, 7, 33, 37, 39, 63, 90, 125-128, 130, 132, 156
sexism, 33, 39, 107, 109, 116, 143
sharecroppers, 8
Sheppard, T.G., 4
Sherrill, Billy, 60
Siverstien, Shel, 112
sin, 36, 52, 63, 137
Sizer, Sandra, 29-30
Snow, Hank, 150
soft-shell country music, 13
SoundScan, 79-80
Southern Baptists, 144
Southern Gospel Music, 26-28, 30-31, 83, 117; history of, 26-28
Southern Rock, 76-77, 99
Spencer, Jon Michael, 3, 25, 110
Spirituals, 25-26, 31-32, 38, 74
"Stand by Your Man," 37, 38, 100, 135, 154
Stewart, Gary, 38
Strait, George, 12, 76, 78, 95-96, 145, 152, 153, 154
Stuart, Marty, 58
suicide, 55
Sylvia, 37

Index

Talbert, Charles 73
Taylor, James, 76
theodicy, 25-26, 40, 83
theology, 2, 3, 5-6, 41, 50, 89, 98-99, 104, 110, 144, 153; defined, 5-6
theomusicology, 3
Thompson, Hank, 39, 104
Tichi, Cecelia, 13, 15-19, 55-56, 59
Tillich, Paul, 6
Tillis, Pam, 132
Tillman, Floyd, 35
Tippin, Aaron, 100, 142, 151
Travis, Randy, 4, 12, 67, 96, 151
Travolta, John, 12
Trevino, Rick, 4
Trio, 83
Tritt, Travis, 67, 99, 150, 151
Tubb, Ernest, 34, 35
Twain, Shania, 125-128, 135, 143
Twitty, Conway, 126, 132

Urban Cowboy, 12, 35
urban migration, 9, 36, 82, 121
urbanization, 34, 36, 81
ultimate concern, 6, 35, 111, 113, 115
upper-middle class, 67, 112

Van Zandt, Townes, 83

videos, 1, 78-79, 89, 125-128, 131
Viorst, Judith, 133
Vonnegut, Kurt, 59

Wagoner, Porter, 124
Walker, Clay, 147
Wayne, John, 89
Wealth, 50-51, 150
Wells, Kitty, 38-39, 104, 135, 143
Wet Willie, 77
Whisnant, David, 15-17
White, Bryan, 100
white trash, 44
Whitley, Keith, 24, 89, 130
Whitman, Walt, 16
Williams, Hank, 1, 4, 11, 15, 34, 37, 41, 42, 43-59, 60, 61, 62, 67, 71, 77, 83, 89, 95, 98, 104, 111, 112, 115, 123, 130, 141, 142, 144, 145, 146-147, 148, 150, 153, 154, 155; as Luke the Drifter, 49, 50, 98 childhood, 44-45; death of, 48; gospel songs, 49, 50; marriage, 46, 47
Williams, Hank, Jr., 46-47, 58
working class, 8-9, 19, 21, 28-29, 34, 66, 104, 106, 12, 116-118, 142-143

Wynette, Tammy, 37, 38, 77, 102, 103, 115-118, 123, 130, 135, 143, 154

Yearwood, Trisha, 132, 133-134, 143
Yoder, John Howard, 1
Young, Neil, 83
"Your Cheatin' Heart," 37, 53